Michelle —

Thank you for reading.
You have no idea
how much young
writers like me
appreciate it.
— Maggie Wang
9/14/2019

RETURN ON INVESTMENT

5¢

BY MAGDALENA WAZ

RETURN ON INVESTMENT

A NOVEL

Magdalena Waz

Fiction Attic Press. Burlingame, CA

RETURN ON INVESTMENT

A Fiction Attic Press Book / September 2016

Published by Fiction Attic Press
Burlingame, California

This is a work of fiction. Names, characters, places, and incidents are a product of the author's imagination. Any resemblance to actual people, living or dead, or to businesses, companies, events, institutions, or locales is completely coincidental.

Cover design by Michelle Richmond with Canva
Milk bottle art by Daniel Boddicker

Library of Congress Cataloging-in-Publication Data

Waz, Magdalena
Return on Investment/ Magdalena Waz.
ISBN: 978-0-991-14998-8 (paperback)
ISBN: 978-1-945-75301-5 (ebook)
1. Satire-Fiction. 2. Literary – Fiction. 3. Contemporary Women – Fiction.

2016947684

Printed in the United States of America
Fiction Attic Press
P.O. Box 137
Burlingame, CA/94011
www.fictionattic.com

CHAPTER ONE

Laurie

Her Tuesday morning appointment is a simple one. A mother of three who just doesn't have much interest in the process anymore. She walks around in a perpetual state of pregnant: palms on the small of her back, fingers facing down, a bulge of a stomach artificially extended forward. Every morning, she opens the door for her breast pump, and she's got eyes that ask, "How much longer?" There's a gentle cooing coming from her infant's crib by the large picture window.

"Is the canister ready or do you need me to wash it?" she asks the mom, who makes room on the wool couch, scratchy later on their shins.

"Wash it, but you can use the tub if it's easier."

Laurie locates the canister in the kitchen. It's just like all the others. They've become popular items at farmers markets both as kitschy vases and as sterile containers which look great in glass door refrigerators. When empty, they're light like aluminum, but filled with milk, they expose the flimsiest wire handle; the spout is not so great for pouring. It'll fit better in the tub than in the sink overflowing with yesterday's dishes. Maybe it would be polite to offer to stack them neatly in the dishwasher. Laurie doesn't know if her duties can include light housekeeping. She's technically scheduled for the hour, but this mom hasn't required the whole time in weeks.

In the bathroom, the lighting fixtures are new and modern, matching the view of Chicago's skyline out the little window. Trump Tower gleams a little too sharply against its matte neighbors. If she turns her head, the whole building disappears in a collage of clouds. Before she begins the work of rinsing out the canister in steaming hot water, she looks in the mirror to adjust her expression into one of pleasant acceptance. They say online that a bad attitude around the mother changes the milk, so she pulls the corners of her lips up and softens the creases around her eyes by rubbing her temples. Usual imperfections catch her eye: the pores on her nose, the unplucked light eyebrows, and blonde hair tinged green and parted down the middle. The top of her smock has a few milk spots on it, and she considers doing some spot cleaning. Every minute in the bathroom, though, is a minute wasted from the mom's perspective. Now, that kind of thinking will get her good Yelp reviews if they ever let her business onto Yelp. Productivity is key here. Laurie is not a slacker.

Back in the living room, Laurie sits down opposite Flora and watches her unsnap the buttons of her cardigan and then the hooks of her shirt. It happens in slow-motion for Laurie each time because she is both eager to begin work and disturbed by how many women are willing to expose their breasts to a near stranger for the sake of making sure they're getting it right. Maybe it's not so cynical; maybe Laurie is a companion. Or maybe that's not right either.

When they're exposed, round and breast-like, she stretches her arms over her head, tries to work the stiffness out of her back, and leans in to do her job. She has to remember to hide her teeth and not leave bite marks. Breasts bruise easily, and sometimes, they stay that way. It's something she needs to incorporate into her new ad outlining her now sizable experience. This mom likes to stabilize herself by grabbing the pump's shoulders and trying to make small talk, but it doesn't come in the form of questions anymore. Now, Flora only speaks of her friends, where they had lunch the other day, where the good sales are, how the older kids are doing at school. When she wanted to know about Laurie the first few times, they got spills when Laurie tried to speak. It's a relief for the mom to not have to hook up pumps and corks and cups and flanges once a week, no matter the mess and the initial discomfort. Laurie can feel it in the way Flora's back curves into a natural slump. But this time is a little different. Laurie sucks hard enough that her teeth and her cheeks meet painfully.

"It's not really working," Laurie says.

"Try clamping down harder. I'm not feeling any suction."

"I tried. It didn't work." Laurie lifts her face, brushes some limp hair away, and looks up. "Is this the end?"

"It might be."

"Well," Laurie says, taking her smock off. "You'll have to call me if anything changes." She pauses. "I mean. It's a little early for you to run dry." She notes the panic in the mom's face and adjusts, "but nothing totally unexpected." As she climbs down from the couch and walks barefoot to the door, she adds, "Say hello (and goodbye) to the children and your husband when they're back home."

"My husband was never too excited to talk about you. Thought this was crossing some sort of line." The mom has her bra back on and is wrapping herself in a blanket.

"I know that game," Laurie laughs, thinking of the relief and dread that will cross Mark's face when she tells him she lost another client.

"I've got some more pregnant friends. Sylvia is due in a month, and Annie the month after that. You've met them."

"Didn't one of them...walk in on us?" It sounds so silly to Laurie when she puts it like that, as if this was somehow illicit.

"Yeah. That was Sylvia."

By now, they're both standing at the door.

"It was good getting to know you," Laurie says not knowing how else to indicate an exit.

"We might see each other again. It's just a hiccup. Here, let me write you a check." In the note section, the mom writes "lactation expenses."

¢

She walks to her second appointment through Wicker Park where babies in strollers accompany runners as their cheerleaders and extra resistance. The fountain has been off for weeks and is accumulating the litter and dried leaves of a city getting colder and crisper every day. Laurie anticipates what it will look like in the spring when the snow melts, a deep stain in the fountain's bowl that can only be pressure washed by an army of people hired to make the city beautiful for summer visitors. But Laurie is not complaining; the sun is out, and what's left of the leaves is red and orange, casting everyone in a warmth which might disappear at any moment.

This second appointment, not far from the first, is only the third in an initial series of ten. Perhaps naturally, the mom is still nervous and claws angry marks into her own arms as Laurie begins her work.

"It will hurt or just feel really foreign the first few times," she says in between mouthfuls with what she thinks is a soothing voice.

"I know. It's just weird. Maybe we can try again tomorrow? Don't think I can tolerate a whole hour, but I'll pay you for all of it," the mom says, reaching for her wallet on the coffee table. "It's a beautiful day outside. You should enjoy it."

Laurie considers leaving half of the money on the black and spotless kitchen counter. She's trying to total her projected monthly earnings, but she can't account for all the squeamish moms who back out at the last minute, or the ones who run dry, or the ones who run out of patience and demand visits more than once a day—that's where Laurie draws the line; she's not a machine.

¢

The third appointment is not really an appointment at all but a voicemail cancellation from a mom who forgot she was going on vacation, but don't worry, she's got her electric unit with her. She'll write when she's back in town, if it's necessary at all. Not surprising. She was the kind of person who never made eye contact. Preferred a text message to a conversation. Plus, she was a sweater. Beads of it formed uniformly on her face and rolled down her chin to threaten Laurie underneath until the danger got dabbed away.

¢

After dinner, Laurie and Mark are relaxing on the cramped loveseat. It's not that their apartment is too small for bigger furniture, it's the awkward layout of it plus the hand-me-down nature of all their stuff. The kitchen is packed way into the back of the apartment with a sunny windo—all that makes the space tolerable. But the sunlight can't reach the dining room on account of the useless wall separating the two rooms. And because it's dark, bare, and too big, Laurie and Mark don't spend any time in there, preferring the equally-sized but less dark living room, which has the drawback of being too close to the tiny bedroom of their on-again, off-again roommate, who is off right now, pretending to backpack out west but is really just staying with a cousin who lured him with the prospect of free food in exchange for baby-sitting. The front door of the apartment is in the dining room. Guests entering don't know whether to turn left or right and consider the dining room to be more of a foyer than anything else, judging by the mountain of shoes, the coat rack.

Laurie has theoretical plans: knock out the wall between the dining room and the kitchen to let in more light, use the now-open space to house a new island equipped with bar stools, turn the dining room into a living area, move the wall between the living room and tiny bedroom to expand the bedroom and turn the living room into a small office/den. The only thing she wouldn't change is her and Mark's bedroom. It's at the same end of the apartment as the kitchen and gets good light. They have photos on the wall to remind them of their summer abroad in London, and their bedspread was Laurie's graduation gift from her mother, all of its starburst colors vibrant and masking the starkness of their simple pine furniture. Every morning, she makes the bed, even when their floor is a sea of dirty clothes. Never mind the fact that London's summer abroad put her another ten thousand in debt and that she hasn't seen her mother since graduation when she's only a five hour train ride away.

"You know, breast milk is a restaurant delicacy now," Mark says without looking away from his laptop. "The FDA is not too happy about it because there's really no way to regulate the supply. What would the legislation have to look like? How could you get away with testing moms before they provided milk? What would you test them for?"

"You can interview me for a piece on it. I can be an expert with inside knowledge."

"I'd call it a conflict of interest at the very least, or advertising at the worst."

There's Mark's discomfort with mixing public and private spheres.

He tells her she smells like powdered baby. It makes him sleepy.

She doesn't notice the smell but her breasts swell with what she's been calling sympathy milk, probably a salty brine if it's anything at all. She can feel their new bulk when she leans in for what she thinks could be a spontaneous kiss, but his mouth is already open around his next words.

He asks, "Did you brush your teeth yet?"

"Yes," she replies and moves away from him to the opposite end of the couch.

"You taste milky all the time. It's like it seeped in."

He's scrolling through news stories and looking for an item that might spark a blog post more removed from his day to day life, she suspects. He wants to be a pundit, but an honest one, and he wants more hits on his YouTube channel, but Laurie thinks that he doesn't know how to sell what he thinks is his original brand of good humor and insightful commentary. She offered to write his website copy and run his twitter account, but they never sat down to cobble together the details. He found a job, started falling asleep around 10:30 p.m. to feel "rested" in the mornings, even though she sees the insomnia bags under his eyes right before he leaves with his coffee in a travel mug she bought him as a birthday gift. It seems too easy for him, and on most days she wants to grab him by the bony shoulders, shake him not too lightly, and ask, "Why aren't you working for it?" But he'll think it an idiotic question, or he'll lie and tell her he is working for it, just in the evenings.

"Yeah, maybe I've got to get in on that black market. Start stealing milk, selling it by the ounce." She shifts her weight on the inherited couch. A metal spring grinds against itself. "Might pay a little better, and I think the first mom is almost all dried up. We had to cut our session short today."

"You don't have to tell me anything about their flavors or shapes."

She rolls her eyes. "You're the one who brought it up."

Mark goes to bed without a word, without a kiss, and she knows this is now officially a new pattern of theirs, going to bed at different times so that they can avoid talking about the fact that sex is not happening. Not a lack of attraction. Laurie wouldn't say that. She's like the middle-aged executive, complaining about the stress of a job, preferring the intimacy and usefulness of a massage to the intimacy and uselessness of sex. It's normal, too, for there to be a growing apart in times of stress. That is at least what David told her when she asked if this was the beginning of the end.

Laurie googles breast milk in restaurants once she's sure the lights are off in their bedroom. She finds a cookbook and a forum dedicated to recipes and restaurants which include breast milk on a secret but not so secret menu. She wonders if this is information that might belong in her Craigslist ad and the information she shares with local women on baby forums as part of an effort to expand the market. In the laptop's night glow, she opens her word document to edit the text she's been using to attract clients for the past three months. She makes changes in bold to review in the morning, like a real editor.

~~**Recent College Grad Seeks Position as Human Breast Pump**~~
Experienced Milk Extraction Professional Seeks New Clients

Why have a machine do the work of a human? The world has gone the way of the self-checkout for too long. More and more people lose their jobs to impersonal and poorly-programmed computers every day. And more often than not, these machines don't save us time because they cannot intuit what we need.

As a breast pump, I know what to do when you feel pain or discomfort. The process of extracting breast milk is something that I understand. In fact, I can also help newly-initiated mothers with the stress and pain of producing milk.

In addition to initial consultation, I offer ~~I cannot meet with you every time your breasts need to be emptied near the beginning. I would say that~~ extraction services ~~are~~ for the established producer who knows when she'll need me (usually between the hours of 8am and 8pm). I charge 40 dollars per session and offer a prepaid discount.

~~Think of your plastic breast pump as the sterile hospital and me as a friendly midwife who has a kind of spiritual connection to the art of keeping moms and babies happy.~~ [too new age-y]

Please email for a no-obligation consultation. I live near Wicker Park, Logan Square, and Ukrainian Village, but will travel to you wherever you may be.

--Laurie, The Human Breast Pump

The career center at Eaton College (like Oberlin, but smaller and more obscure) kept imploring her to create demand, to spin lack of opportunity into something better. So she invented a profession that didn't need to exist in the first place. Mark asked during the unemployed month of July, "Don't they have little plastic suction cups for that?"

Yeah, but the little plastic suction cup couldn't also be a friend or at the very least a silent companion. And at the beginning of September when she hit her peak in breast milk extraction, Mark found himself asking if she might not need to hire employees soon.

Before bed, she brushes her teeth for three minutes with the help of her phone's timer. A film of something she calls organic matter forms on the back of her incisors, and it doesn't come loose when she touches it with her tongue. The bottom teeth feel cleaner, but she brushes them just as vigorously.

¢

She knows to target the second mom first. Being an irregular producer yields some benefits in that Laurie doesn't have to answer questions about there being too little milk at the end of the session. Laurie is unsure about how much money to invest in this venture, so her first attempt involves an insulated coffee mug and a vinyl lunch bag she's had since high school. She's always held that the best schemes require the simplest setups.

Mom number two opens the door for her with a creased forehead. She's cleared a space on the couch, prepared the canister, put her six-month-old daughter down for a nap. Very professional.

"Let's try this again. Remember, there's no pressure," Laurie says, leaving her bags at the door. She pretends there's coffee in the mug and takes a sip in order to justify setting it down on the coffee table. "Today, try to close your eyes the whole time. If it helps you to adjust, pretend that I'm the pump you used before you hired me."

To mask the sounds, Laurie pulls out her phone and searches for something quiet without vocals and settles on a classical station. When she hears it, the mom sighs and says, "That might help."

Laurie looks up to make sure her eyes are closed and makes an attempt on the left breast. Soft milk bursts into her mouth, and she has to remind herself not to swallow. After she collects what feels like a mouthful, she deposits it into the canister.

"Am I doing better this time?" the mom asks.

"Yes. I think closing your eyes is really helping."

The second mouthful, a little smaller than the first, goes into the empty coffee mug. The pump checks to make sure she's not arousing suspicion. It's quiet except for a mournful clarinet solo, a car rolling down the street, and their breathing. So, not quiet at all actually. Peaceful might be the word. The work is steady, and when she's finished, the breast is noticeably limper and both the canister and the thermos are over halfway full of the milky stuff.

"Thank you so much," the mom sighs. "I've really wanted to breast feed Greta, but she had trouble latching and every article I read made me feel guilty about it." She frowns, shrugs. "Anyway, I'm glad I found you."

"It's my pleasure. Anything to keep your baby happy and healthy," Laurie says as she tightens the cap on her thermos and sticks it into her lunch bag.

¢

She finds the restaurant on Yelp. She takes the blue line downtown and emerges from the subway with a cold jar of milk. When she got home from seeing mom number two, she transferred the contents of the thermos into a mason jar and stuck it in the fridge. Mark wasn't home. She wouldn't tell him until she succeeded anyway. The restaurant is trendy enough to pay a high price for a strange ingredient. All she has to do is look respectable, look like the milk is hers.

"I'm here to see the executive chef," she says to the host who is switching out the wine lists in their leather cases. "I've heard he's interested in a special kind of ingredient."

He looks down at Laurie's baggy t-shirt, loose jeans meant to indicate postpartum but a wealthy kind where her flats still look new and her hair is clean. "I'll find the manager for you," he says with a knowing smile. The back wall is covered in a wallpaper with a raised black velvet design. The wood is dark, and the light fixtures are caged Edison bulbs. She imagines a breast milk cocktail: a cold froth on top of the heaviness of vermouth, a hint of rye, a dash of trendy mint bitters. She'd serve it in a jar or a bowl with a long silver cappuccino spoon for stirring the froth in.

A round man in a red t-shirt spotty with moth holes walks into the dining room and says, "I believe you have some extra breast milk you'd like to sell me?" Only the important and wealthy can afford to look so disheveled and be so direct.

"I do. I've only got twelve ounces today, but I can guarantee deliveries once a week." Laurie is afraid she's being too forward, but she doesn't know how to tiptoe around the issue. What she's doing is illegal according to a cursory search of Chicago's Department of Public Health website, but she wants this money, and she knows breast milk is a delicacy worth sampling. "I can guarantee this batch is freshly pumped, stored in the fridge in a sanitized glass container until I transported it here."

"Future batches? Will you freeze them? Will they have to be boiled?"

"I'm not sure that there are food safety standards established for breast milk outside of the advice given to new moms," Laurie said. "If you're not serving it right away---"

"The chef will know all of that then. He's got a newborn." The man takes the jar Laurie offers and holds it up to the dim light filtering from outside through old lace curtains. "Good color. Looks clean. How much?"

"Seven an ounce."

"Five."

"Six. It's not easy getting even that much out of a breast."

Instead of a verbal agreement, he pulls crumpled bills from his pocket and straightens them out against his jeans. "It'll always be cash, and when they tell us to stop, we will. This restaurant won't close, but we'll have to comply." He looks over at the host. "And from now on, just announce yourself by name to the host. He'll know where to send you."

Laurie takes that as her cue to say, "I'm Alice. Very nice to meet you both." She shakes some hands, bundles the money and sticks it into a coin purse.

He unscrews the cap on the jar and lifts the contents to his nose.

"I'm Joseph. See you on Monday?"

"Yes."

¢

With the seventy two dollars in her pocket, Laurie prepares a feast for dinner. Salmon filets coated in black pepper and black sea salt flavored with lemon and rosemary, a hearty bread, salad overflowing with heirloom tomatoes and peppers of all shapes and sizes. For dessert, she'll serve an artisanal ice cream with real vanilla and bourbon.

Mark comes home from six hours of data entry and kisses her hello. He says, "Not too milky tonight."

Laurie sits down across from him and says, "That's not really the best way to thank me for this feast, but I only had the one woman today."

Mark's eyes narrow as he looks at their dinner. Candlelight makes it glow even warmer. Laurie had hoped that the food's volume would make him forget to ask the question he remembers next.

"How did you pay for all of this then?"

"I sold some of her milk to Avalanche & Amble downtown."

"It worked? This is black market breast milk money?"

"Yes. And there's more where that came from." She picks up a fork and flakes off a bite of the filet. It's not too dry, perfectly seasoned. "I gave them a fake name and everything."

¢

In bed, she checks her texts before Mark asks her to turn off the bedside lamp. There's one, and it's brief from Flora: "All dried up. Sorry :(." That doesn't leave her with much of anything to do tomorrow or the next day. She'll siphon off some more milk from her supplier, and calculate the kind of money she'll be making until they all get caught.

CHAPTER TWO

David

The hotel bars David prefers are sumptuous and velvety. He likes them better still if there's a man playing piano on a low stage. Tonight, there's a man playing a piano on a low stage, and David taps his credit card on the wraparound bar in time with the music, which masks the idle conversation of hotel bar patrons at once put together and bedraggled by endless travel. David doesn't have cufflinks, but that's not his look. He prefers to play the disheveled musician with a uniform, dark stubble and glinting hazel eyes into which he injects a smile when he sees any woman alone with a tiny purse.

The bartender knows him. She rolls her eyes probably because she sees that he's wearing the same dark jeans and plush flannel with the sleeves hiked up to reveal what David considers to be sinewy arms. Laurie tells him to play up his "exotic" features by letting his hair grow out in loose waves, but he likes the feel of a buzz cut (like rattlesnake skin) even if it means that he looks less obviously Latin American.

"What'll it be this week?"

"Any reasonably-priced scotch with a pretty large ice cube in it." He doesn't have to impress the bartender because he knows he doesn't stand a chance with someone his own age. When this bartender looks at him, he feels her cynicism. The bartender wouldn't want anyone like him for more than a few dates, and what he's on the market for is something more.

"Just give me the name of the scotch you want."

"I don't know. Does Dewar's have a nice color?"

"Sure." She turns and takes her time near the other end of the bar. It's a Wednesday and too far past the dinner hour for there to be a rush, and the only people left in the place are the mid-week daters without responsibilities at home, lonely travelers, and the hunters like David. He only has the budget for one drink (two if anyone accepts his advances). The rest of his bank account is dedicated to some quick groceries (he's not a cook, which works against him in relationships) and student loans, automatic payments on an accelerated plan.

The woman he spots walking in from the well-lit lobby has unnaturally straight hair and a narrow face that ends in a trendy point which accentuates her laugh lines. She scowls now, though, and flips open the envelope-sized silver clutch under her bare arm to check for something. Satisfied, she closes it back up, walks straight for the bar and sits a respectful two seats away from David, pulling her lips into a pale line of a smile in greeting, not as a concrete offer.

He smiles back and turns to the bartender to say, "Whatever the lady orders, put it on my tab." The words feel slimy in his mouth, and in his embarrassment, he tries to hand over his card and take his drink in one motion.

"You mean me?" the woman asks.

"Yes. I'm sorry. I should have introduced myself first instead of doing it like they do in Humphrey Bogart movies." He sticks out his hand. "I'm David Solano."

"Gertrude," she says, taking his hand into a silky handshake that makes him feel like he's the one with a dead, scaly fish for a hand. "I appreciate the offer, but I would like to pay for my own drink."

And the bartender doesn't even laugh. She's been witness to worse rejections than this one. Professionally, she takes Gertrude's order of a gin & tonic.

"That's no problem at all. I'm sorry if I was a little forward."

"It's what I've come to expect in this kind of bar," she laughs, and it makes David feel less like a predator. She puts her elbows on the bar and inspects her nails. "I was going to head out somewhere, but I don't know one bar from another down here, so I figured I'd save myself the trouble of putting on a coat."

"Yeah. No offense to this classy establishment, but every bar

around here is the same. You're not missing out by staying in."
This week, David is thinking he'll play the knowledgeable local
instead of the sad traveller.

"And I get gin & tonics everywhere anyway so I don't need
anything special going on behind the bar."

"But you do look like you're anticipating a nice night."

"Well, my mother always taught me to go out in public
dressed and painted in case I ran into my future husband at the
grocery store."

David jolts at the word husband. Maybe this is also exactly
what Gertrude is looking for. She's testing him to see how serious he might be. The statement gives him enough courage to ask
her to dance. She pauses before saying yes, and in that pause
David almost has her written off. Nothing in her expression
clues him in to the fact that she could be falling in love. He
doesn't want to be a fling or a story she tells her best friend
when she gets back home. But there's nothing to do but see the
project through to the end and take the risk that it will flop.

She puts half of her body against his in an almost intimate
embrace, and they sway to the music while the bartender and
pianist watch. It's not the kind of Wednesday night this bar sees
often, the blooming of a young love. They dance this way
through two songs, and Gertrude breaks the spell by insisting
she isn't drunk. She's barely had two sips of her drink down
here, but her arms are a loose flubber to David. When she removes her arm from the crook of his neck, he feels how damp
his shirt is there, and he can't tell whose sweat it is.

"Let's go back," she says.

Later, they're undressed, under the covers, and David's arm
is falling asleep under Gertrude's bare ribs. Her dress was easy
to remove, and it lost its shape the second she was out of it. His
flannel buttons gave her some trouble. Their size was all off, and
the stitching around the buttonholes was fraying.

"I've never done this before," she says.

"Me neither."

¢

David is on an old and decommissioned school bus counting women wearing flip-flops with large stuffed penis attachments sticking straight up. He won't call them erect because they're plush, as stiff as a teddy bear's arm. The woman nearest him lifts her legs up, leaning back in her seat, attempting to flop her penises around, asking him, "What do you think of these guys?"

"Well, they're not anatomically correct," he says. It's late, and his work with these women is almost done. They don't look like they're going to tip big. They're the wrong kind of drunk. So there's not that urgency to play along he usually feels. Club Superior is not their last stop. The club itself looks like a private karaoke bar with narrow black-lit hallways painted dark, chic colors. There are five private rooms upstairs and an expansive, public bar downstairs. These woman spend about two hours in private rooms ordering bottle service until they're ready to mingle downstairs with the regular patrons, and then they go on to the next spot, usually a busier club, and after that, he's not sure. All he has to do is make sure that no woman wanders too far away from her party and that the bus or limo is full when they're ready to move on. Honestly, David doesn't think much about their next destination because their next destination is some other guy's responsibility, but sometimes he wonders if that other guy understands this post is a noble one and not some easy way to snag a lady. There is no fun in it, for either party here. No hunt, no serendipity, no romance.

"Maybe your penis is the penis that isn't anatomically correct," she says, scrutinizing his face to see if he'll want to fight over it.

"I guess we'll never know." He turns from her and asks, "Where's our maid of honor?" He consults his sheet. "Jessica? Can I get you up here?"

When Jessica walks up from the back of the bus, David confirms that they're ready to leave, makes her initial the guest list, offers her another copy of the receipt and thanks her for choosing Club Superior as one of their destinations. She nods, reaches into a pocket of her denim shorts, and pulls out a crumpled twenty dollar bill.

"Thanks for getting us on the bus!" she blurts out, a little drunk but certainly not the worst he's seen.

¢

People out this late don't look like they're either coming or going, and David appreciates that ambiguity. On the blue line, it's mostly people with suitcases, and he sometimes catches himself checking addresses on the luggage tags to figure out who he's dealing with: a native Chicagoan moving for the first time through the night city, a backpacker from a different country taking advantage of a cheap red eye fare, a strange commuter who divides her time between two cities – one where she has a home and one where she has a job. No matter their origin or destination, three in the morning catches people looking down at their feet listening to darkness's echoes and refusing to meet his eyes.

Modest single family homes sporting facades of decorative brick make up his neighborhood. His street is quiet with flickering light. He sees it twice a week this way, and no matter the season, he hears the creaking and cracking of fences alongside the hum of electricity running through the alleys. He rents a basement from an older couple, enters his apartment through their laundry room. But the door leading up into the main house is respectfully closed. He makes a green tea at home in the half-dark of the stove light and hopes in the morning that his voice is less hoarse. All night he's been yelling over the pulse of music to make sure that his charges are satisfied with the room, the drinks, the volume of the music – always louder.

He remembers a litany of questions he's been asked tonight:

"David. Is that your real name?"

"David, do people rent you for bachelorette parties? Or do you come with the venue?"

"David, how does your girlfriend feel about you being around hundreds of beautiful women each week?

"David, how does your mother feel about your job?"

His bed is raised high over an orange linoleum floor from the 1950s when the house was built. The mattress he bought new, but even though he could spend all day in it, he preserves the metal springs and sits on the cold floor glued straight to the concrete foundation with his back propped against an equally orange couch borrowed from Barb and Morris, the owners, when they noticed he had almost no furniture, having come straight from a dorm. Feeling around under the couch for a pen, he finds pieces of waterlogged dictionary pages, old and peeling from the floor. The page he sees first is an f page: fatal, fatalism, fatalist, fatalistic, fatality, fatally, Fata Morgana, Fate, fated, fateful, father. He wonders in that brief moment how many words exist that make some reference to death. He wonders, too, how many times this basement has flooded and when it's due for another. Barb invites David up for tea and cookies from time to time and says, "Morris, he built this house with his own two hands. We were the first ones on the block you know. Brick by brick we had to do it because even back then houses weren't cheap." Her voice is clear with only a slight hoarseness at the end of her sentences. Even in her 70s, Barb wears a string of pearls on top of a pastel cotton sweater. Her skirts, though long and pleated, are always pressed, and she still fidgets with her wedding ring as if it were brand new.

¢

He slips the rent into their mail slot, which empties into their hall closet. In an unmarked envelope, he arranges bills from smallest to largest. Barb and Morris are careful money managers. They probably appreciate David's attention to detail, the clean way he handles money. At the end of the month, he usually has enough tip money for rent, and his direct deposit wages cover the rest of his living expenses, which includes the loan payment.

The loan payment is bigger than his rent. The loan payment is what he can't defer, the dog that will keep snapping at his heels, herding him into the jobs he would prefer not to take.

¢

Before he leaves for work on a Saturday in September, David walks up the poured concrete steps of the house to drop off his rent. After the mail slot clinks shut, Barb opens the door, and through the screen says, "Come into the front room for a second. Do you have a minute?"

He demonstrates some frustration with a pointed look at his watch but enters anyway.

"Where are you headed?"

"To work."

Barb looks out the window at the accelerating sunset and then looks down at her own watch. David knew this moment would come, and he's surprised that it's already been three months of middle of the night screen door squeaks, and Barb hasn't asked. She knows where his family is from (Naperville, most recently). She knows how many siblings he has (two, both younger). And she knows he's allergic to cats. But she hasn't asked yet where he works. "Is it far to where you work?"

"No. About twenty minutes on the blue line, and I usually walk the rest of the way from the Chicago stop."

"You a bartender? Sit down," she says, patting the plastic encased furniture.

"Yes, I'm sort of a bartender." He backs up toward the door without taking his eyes off Barb. He doesn't want her to think that he's impolite, but she's looking at his clothes (frayed jeans over scuffed slip-ons, a flannel with the sleeves rolled up to the elbows–too casual for the kind of bartender she might be imagining).

"I'm more of a manager type working behind the scenes. I deal with guest lists and making sure that everyone's having a good time, but I do work in a bar. I don't have to be there until a little after we open, but I stay well after close." Talking too fast. His words are sliding all over each other. Every explanation piling onto the last one until they're just shy of believable.

"And it's good money? I almost never see you leave during the week, and I just want to make sure everything's all right down there."

As the clock nearest him settles into the seven o'clock position, the first cuckoo starts to blurt its song, and when it's finished, the other three clocks follow one by one loud enough to drown out anything else Barb could have said. David nods to answer the question, but knows it won't be enough for Barb. Trapped by the sound of the clocks, he can't stand up to say his goodbyes until it is dead silent again and just the ticking resumes. Barb taps her knee with an impatient finger. She's waiting for more, another outpouring of information.

"Yeah. Everything is fine. Thank you for asking."

¢

As he walks along Irving Park, David lets the sunset blind him. Yes, he manages guest lists, but the women on these guest lists generally wear lewd party hats or shoes and harass him until he takes his shirt off or plants a chaste kiss on the bride-to-be's cheek with the suggestion that it could be more if she wasn't spoken-for. The official job description makes it possible for him to leverage it nicely on a resume ("Special Events Coordinator"), but there's only so much imprecise and managerial language he can use before he has to admit that he babysits bachelorette parties. What's worse, perhaps, is that he doesn't have very many stories to tell. He gets in, does his job, gets out, and spends the rest of his time comparing himself to his old classmates on Facebook. Their children in some cases twirling in clever costumes at parties specifically for young people with children. He wonders what it takes these days to become a public intellectual, and he knows that it's more than writing cultural criticism for the school newspaper. Is it cultural criticism if it's consistently written for an audience of about ten? Better than his current blog with an audience of one. His most recent post: "The fastest mode of transportation to and from Wrigley Field is walking (at least from my apartment before, during, and after a Cubs game)." He wrote it on the Addison bus as it vied for a spot back in traffic generated by cars bound for subdivisions in the suburbs.

¢

It's a busy night at Club Superior; three parties at the same time and David finds himself doing more than the usual clearing of drinks and managing the cleaning of each private room.

There's a group playing Scrabble, and they've asked him to join. They wait patiently as David makes his rounds and comes back to their room at the end of the hall to place a word on the board. His letters keep changing because his empty spot at the low coffee table has become the depository for the unwanted Q, Z, J, and X.

"Come on, guys. I know I didn't have these letters when I left." He feigns surprise as he sits down on the floor between Alli and Alex. "You're cheating." Flirty, light voice with no real accusation in it.

"We are not," they say in unison, and it's all part of the fun. They've made a new friend for the night, and he's going to let them win because his job is to make sure they're having a good time. Not that he would win if they left him the string of vowels he was working with before, but he is used to this innocent flirtation, and he's good at keeping it light, which just means smiling often with his naturally straight teeth underneath a wide span of cheekbone.

Monica, the maid of honor, approaches the table, kneels next to David. Her skirt spills beige tulle over her legs. She smells like lavender perfumed vodka. Her face is healthy and clean. Makeup expertly highlights her high cheekbones, her flawless eyebrows. "Thank you for keeping everyone happy. It was a feat getting all these women in the same room together," she whispers in a way that is both apologetic and conspiratorial. The secret here, David assumes, is that she and he are on the same team, both wranglers of the rowdy and sometimes belligerent.

"No problem," he whispers back and turns to place the word "fez" on the board.

"Not a word," says Alli.

"Google it," he answers, getting up and checking his clipboard and watch. "I'll be back in a few."

But he doesn't make it back for another forty five minutes, and by then the board is cleared, Monica is packing away the games into a plastic bin, and it's maybe the first party in weeks that he's almost sad to see go. The rest of the women are toasting each other, toasting the venue, toasting Monica, forgetting all about the impending wedding, although this one isn't for a few weeks. Monica doesn't pause to acknowledge her own name. She's clearing tables, making David's job easier. He can smell a little bit of that perfume still lodged in his nostrils or the room itself, and he wants to tell her to relax and enjoy the party she planned, but he's having trouble relaxing around her. No smooth non sequiturs and confident smiles. Certainly no drinks because that's against company policy. The party went off without a hitch compared to the one next door where a stripper showed up against the bride's wishes and club policy. David has, on a few occasions in his short time at Club Superior, had to tap the nearly naked dancers on the shoulder mid-routine with a bundle of clothes in the other arm, feeling more ridiculous by the second. "Very sorry, but you're going to have to stop now. This is not the type of atmosphere we cultivate here."

"What happened to that Scrabble game?" he asks Monica when he finally catches her attention.

"To David!" Alli yells. "A worthy Scrabble opponent if I ever saw one." She raises her wine glass to him. He smiles back with the clipboard folded to his chest, realizes he looks like a researcher, and lowers his arms to his sides.

"They got bored," Monica says. "But it was Alli's idea, this whole thing. She wanted something tame instead of the strippers and novelty penises."

"I've seen a lot of those. Lots of penis cakes. Lots of immaturity. Gets old quick. I mean, if that's your style. I shouldn't be getting in the way of a good party. I'm supposed to blend into the background. I hope I haven't been obtrusive."

After nodding thoughtfully as if David's long string of words had been an important assessment of the kinds of bachelorette parties he sees in here, she says, "Look. I don't have a date yet for this wedding. It's not for a while, so you don't have to say anything right now. I've been putting off asking and I'm starting to realize that there's no one to wait for."

David sees where this is going, but he's not sure if he wants to be the nobody date at this wedding.

She continues, "I know we don't know each other, but I would really like it if you came with me. The girls all like you, and I don't want to have a situation where they don't like some new boyfriend who I end up dumping a week later. And I don't want a douchebag to show up in Alli's wedding photos for all eternity. The ceremony is really low key at the yacht club right on Lakeshore Drive. You know it."

"You sure Alli is okay with a stranger at her wedding?"

"There will be plenty of strangers. The groom is Blake Crawford."

Without an idea of who that might be, David nods.

"You ever been to the yacht club? It's nice. I snagged the Monroe Harbor location for the ceremony, and the actual party takes place in the cultural center. And I know I've been freaking out about the planning, but the whole wedding party is going to walk through Millennium Park with a photographer of course, which reminds me that I have to make sure to double check that we have our permits," she trails off.

He weighs his options. He could say yes now and take advantage of what seems to be a pretty fancy wedding. He could hold off and say yes later to make it seem like he's not taking advantage. Or he could say yes after looking up Blake Crawford.

Or he could say no because all he knows about this woman is that she's pretty well-organized and has beautiful skin. He considers Gertrude, who was more attractive and more mysterious, but she hadn't called yet, and after a week of silence, he was ready to give up.

"I'll think about it, but I don't see what would keep me from saying yes."

Monica sighs big and says, "Thank you." She steps closer to him and sets her arms on either side of his neck. Her elbows rest stiffly on his shoulders. It's maybe a version of a hug.

"If I say yes, what would you like for me to wear?"

"Early fall colors. The bridesmaids are wearing shades of purple. Everything will be accented with a pale gold. Be fancy casual. I will give you all of this info by email, too. Can you write it down for me?" She has to make her way through the other women to get to her purse in their dedicated coat closet. She disappears from view, and there's a hush when everyone sees that Monica is smiling and that David is still there by the door, taking a break from his job. The women part to let her pass back through the room, trying to maintain a level of acceptable chatter while Monica hands David an iPad and asks him to type in his contact information. It feels less illicit to him this way as he pays attention to the fake keyboard clicking. "Let me email you my info right now," she says when she takes the little machine back.

"So we're all set to be rounded up and stuffed into a party limo?" he asks, remembering his job and the schedule that has him funneling another group in here within half an hour.

"Yes."

David leads them down the back stairs, which are a little rickety but a more direct route to the special party valet area. The name makes it sound more maintained than the cracked concrete alley and harsh streetlight that turns everyone orange, but it's where the limos fit. This party's limo is sleek and low unlike the popular SUV variety with sharp corners and a boxy tail. Everyone thanks David. Monica is last in line, and she gives him an envelope with his name on it and another one of those un-wieldy hugs. He makes her initial the guest list, thanks her, and hands her a copy of the receipt.

"I'll call you soon," she says and turns to go.

In the envelope, David finds fifty dollars with a half sheet of paper wrapped around it. The sheet of paper says, "Thanks for a job well done" in what he can only assume is Monica's handwriting.

¢

Most nights he doesn't go to parties because of work, but when Laurie hosts one on Sunday, he agrees to pop in. Her apartment is a straight shot down Milwaukee Avenue so he takes the bus instead of walking the three miles. He's late because the bus driver is the kind who likes to keep to the printed schedule down to the minute even when there's no traffic, and he can catch a green wave from here to the foot of the skyscrapers. So they wait in front of empty bus shelters for stragglers and brake for yellow lights, or in anticipation of them.

When he gets to her two-flat held together by beige siding, he has to text to be let in because the doorbell is broken—has been broken since she moved in. Her living room, dining room, and kitchen are all bare enough to encourage conversation and mingling. David weaves his way through a small group standing around the gin table to the living room where Laurie has already sat down next to Mark, one of their good friends from college and Laurie's boyfriend or roommate depending on the day.

"How's work treating you?" Mark asks. They both majored in Political Science, had the same professor as honors thesis advis-er, but their competition ended when both arrived in Chicago and could find no job that would admit them into some part of a system they had long-hoped to reform. They aren't aides to an Alderman, they aren't beat writers or even low level administra-tors in the Park District. They are a babysitter (Special Events Coordinator) and a data entry clerk (Processing Assistant).

"Oh, you know. The same penis hats over and over again. Each group thinks it's more original than the last."

"I'd have penis hats at my bachelor party," Mark says. He hints at wanting a wedding more often as the weather turns cold and reminds him that the next year is uncertain. David feels it, too, in the way they're all talking about what it'll be like to file taxes. David notices, though, that there's no specificity to these wedding plans. It's not Laurie he's imagining next to Mark, but anyone willing to be a legitimate adult, words that can't be used to describe someone without an interest in a career.

"But I did almost agree last night to go to a wedding at the yacht club. Kind of as a date and kind of as a stand in for one."

"Oooh. Fancy. But isn't that against some sort of company policy? They're your clients. You can't date them."

"Yeah, but they're only David's clients for one night. After that, they can be his friends," Laurie says. "There are boundaries, but he's not crossing them."

"And this was a board game party, and the woman, Monica, was so uncomfortable asking me, I didn't want to say no, but I also didn't want to say yes right away. She could've thought I was too available. Besides, it gives me a reason to take a weekend off sometime soon, and you know, it's not a bad idea to rub shoulders with the rich kids." David gets up from his spot on the worn rug. "I'm going to get myself a drink."

In the kitchen, he finds himself one clean glass and pours in a eyeballed shot or two of gin (Gertrude Gin) and the rest of the lemonade. He doesn't know anyone smoking on the back deck. When David returns to Laurie and Mark, he finds them next to each other silent on the couch. He forgives their bad manners because they're choosing to spend their party time with him.

Laurie asks, "Who is this Monica woman? Why can't she get a date the normal way?"

David isn't sure whether or not Laurie is asking the right questions, but he knows that there wasn't anything flirty about the invitation, and the exchange of information was sterile like a business transaction. And Monica gave him money that really did feel like a bribe and not a tip. And would he feel less like an escort if he knew he was a last resort? What's the difference? More importantly, he couldn't admit that there was something intoxicating about all of that, so different from what he did on weeknights.

"You and Mark didn't start dating the normal way."

"What do you mean? Yeah, we did." Laurie looks at Mark to confirm.

"I hated you for arguing in the paper that the school should tear down Wilson House. Not all old things should be slated for destruction," Mark says.

"But you don't hate me now."

"I don't hate you now," Mark replies.

David looks at the two of them and wonders if it's the breast milk or something else. But judging by Laurie's face, calculating something through her eye slits, now is not the right time to play therapist with or without Mark around.

He spends the rest of the night worrying and sipping his too bitter concoction, adding ice cubes until what he has is just water. Even a conversation about breast milk and its taste doesn't rouse him from his thoughts until it turns into a fight between Laurie and Mark that has everyone heading out well before midnight. David is the last to leave, but he can't steer Laurie back to a conversation about Monica and her intriguing offer.

He asks her, though, who Blake Crawford is and gets a blank stare.

"Want me to look it up now?" she asks, still enthralled by her smart phone and its endless access to information.

"No. I'd rather just look it up when I get home."

But Laurie isn't listening and in a second she says, "He's a football player for the Bears. This is a serious wedding."

A serious wedding is a dream of his. He wants people to stop and stare when he crawls out of a stretch limo. He wants backup generators for thousands of light bulbs, surrounding an over-sized altar, a real wood dance floor.

CHAPTER THREE

Laurie

Laurie wakes up the morning after the party with something like a hangover although she's been wondering lately about the difference between a hangover and dehydration. To her, they are one and the same: a pounding headache, jelly limbs. She slides out of bed and begins collecting the glasses and mugs left on every available surface. There's the coffee table that moonlights as a TV stand, the bar cart bookcase, the dining table desk, and the stool too short for sitting and too hard for ottomaning. She stacks narrow glasses into wide mugs and tries to carry more than she can handle with shaky hands.

Mark wakes up an hour later and greets her in the kitchen. His hair is already brushed back from his forehead, exposing the dry patches of skin near his hairline. Laurie wonders if they're caused by a vitamin deficiency, or maybe they should have caved and bought a humidifier to place at the foot of their bed. She'd hold her cracked knuckles over the steam spray and steal it from the air, but that's essentially a version of a moist, warm towel, which is essentially free. She remembers the contradictions of last night. They spent half of it shivering into each other for warmth (their version of make-up sex) and the other half at the far ends of the bed, their sweaty limbs hanging low to the ground.

"I shouldn't have made fun of your job like that," he says.

"I don't have one right now." Laurie tries not to slam cupboard doors as she puts away the now dried glasses and mugs.

"Just the one mom and the other gig?"

"That's it."

"It's enough." He squeezes her shoulder (the bony part and not the string of tight sinew near her neck) and adds, "Thanks for cleaning up."

"I mean, I can get more. Just need to re-double my marketing efforts. People give birth all the time. Maybe my mom can call some of her friends from high school and college. I'm sure some of their daughters have kids."

"Your mom wouldn't do that. She hasn't even been to see the new apartment."

Their breakfast is the same kind of modest it was before the new arrangements. Laurie knows they can't get ahead of themselves quite yet, and last week's feast was a misstep. In fact, all the sale did was make up for the fact that she had lost two of her clients last week. Their argument at the party had left her feeling guilty for the meal she cooked to celebrate her new position as milk peddler. Mark told her he would have to ask his parents for rent money this month. She isn't telling him right now, but she's determined to keep things from getting worse for them. And worse in her book is more help from parents. She doesn't want to jinx it, and she doesn't want to feel his disappointment now or inevitably at the end of next month when Thanksgiving will throw off her whole schedule.

"Do you think we live in silence?" she asks.

"No. I think we're both just tired." And after what feels like a silence exaggerated, Mark says, "I've picked up a few more hours at work."

"What about YouTube?"

"It can wait. It's just a web series." Even though Mark isn't trying to sound bitter, Laurie can see the tendons in his neck tighten. His skin is dry down there, too, and rough like an elephant's.

"I think you shouldn't give up on it so quick for data entry. You got some views last week, and I've seen the analytics on your blog. You're pulling in over 500 a month."

"I'm not working for data entry. I'm working for money."

"I told you last night that I'll get the rent money." This time she does slam a cupboard door and immediately regrets the sound it makes.

¢

A week passes before she receives an email from another potential client. During that week, she visits the nervous mom and continues siphoning and selling, doubling her profits with time left over to lead a small job hunt. In addition to looking for new breastfeeding moms, she searches for jobs in social media strategy and copywriting, two jobs vaguely related to a skillset she tried to identify before she left college. The new mom requests a Skype interview. Laurie agrees and picks a time when Mark will be at work, which is every day now. He won't want to see the mom even if she's grainy. And ever since it turned out that he was right about her mom's refusal to help her look for clients, she worried that he could foresee the end of her business and that his presence could jinx her. It starts like any other Skype conversation. One of the two asks, "Can you hear me?"

The other one responds, "Can you see me?"

Both reply, "Yes."

Their signals cross, and they chuckle.

"This is so awkward," the mom says. "But I couldn't think of another safe way to determine whether or not this is something I want. Flora told me about you, by the way. Do you remember her?"

Laurie thinks and remembers Flora as the first mom, the one to lay her off through text message. "Usually, I meet with people in coffee shops for the initial interview, sometimes at home. That's how Flora and I did it, actually." Laurie doesn't mean for this to sound so insulting. She looks down, struggling to maintain eye contact with the woman sitting in her laptop screen. The woman has extensions and artful highlights with wisps of hair cut to shape a face contoured and painted, much like Flora in fact.

"You're offering a very unique service. Why?"

Laurie shrugs. "It's hard to get other jobs, and like my craigslist ad says, I'm interested in taking the sterile parts of motherhood and turning them into something healthy again." It's always enough, this answer, practiced in front of the mirror, although it's very far from the truth.

There are other jobs. Of course, there are. Mark has one. David has one, but Laurie knows herself well enough to know that once she settles on a career path, even if it's data entry, she'll have trouble leaving. That's why she didn't move back home when the time came to graduate.

She schemed with Mark, but his scheming ended when he answered a dry, generic Craigslist ad looking for a tech-savvy data clerk, and after the interview, his justification for giving up was that "the people are nice and the lunches are free."

And part of what hurt was that by giving up, he had won, and she had nothing to show for her dogged hunt for freedom. So instead of giving up, too, she thought that if she stuck it out long enough there would be a bigger payoff than coming in first.

"How do you address the saliva?"

"Most women and midwives agree that germs transmitted through my saliva have certain fortifying properties. Their babies get sick less often, and I've been tested for all communicable diseases." A boilerplate response for a question she hears from new moms and David every time they start to think a little harder about the mechanics of it all. It also doesn't matter whether or not it's true. The disease part, of course. Laurie isn't interested in getting these kids seriously sick, but her spit is just water as far as she's concerned.

"Can we run a trial? I can see how you do it, and we can see if my baby takes to milk that comes from your mouth," she asks and checks her watch. "I have to run, but how do you feel about tomorrow afternoon at three?"

"But I will ask that you pay a discounted rate of—"

"We can discuss the money when you get here. I'll email you my address."

¢

To meet this mother, Laurie puts on yoga pants she generally sleeps in and a colorful windbreaker with her hair already in a high ponytail. Recurring trips to Avalanche & Amble require a certain kind of ease moving through expensive air. This mom, too, doesn't want her to be a fresh college graduate with the messy hair and the crooked glasses and the body shapeless as a blob of molasses because a gym membership and all of its associated costs would clear out her savings in a few short mouse clicks. She read an infographic about picking the right running shoes just last week. One day that knowledge might come in handy, when she has a dry, even, and springy track to run circles around.

The El ride is short. California to Damen where the mom lives above a boutique decorated in birch bark and gold. Laurie puts the block on her list of places she'll one day inspect with Mark, when it's time to invest in property instead of new business ventures. She adjusts her purse on her shoulder and punches a code into a sleek box next to the unassuming door. A block away, the Kennedy cuts its diagonal scar across the city. She can hear the rushing sounds of tires on the concrete and wonders about depreciation.

A harsh voice from inside the box asks, "Yes?"

"It's Laurie from Craigslist and the Skype interview?"

There's a prolonged buzzing in response. Laurie reaches for the door handle and disappears up the stairs.

The lighting is understated and soft, even in the hallway. The door is blue gray and slightly ajar; Laurie prods it open with a finger to expose a sunny apartment with one of those industrial views that can really look glamorous when framed by walnut and glass. The place looks, predictably, like one of Laurie's favorite design catalogues exploded. Just last week, when feeling particularly low, Laurie had taken a walking tour of Chicago's design district just north of the river to daydream. This apartment was what she saw too often in the raised window displays. The number one property on Laurie's never-articulated house hunting list: the Mies buildings at 860-880 North Lake Shore Drive. Gleaming black steel and glass towers high above the smooth lake from where she could watch the curve of the Drive as it disappears north.

"Is this the kind of canister you wanted?" the mother asks. "I ran it through the dishwasher." She's sitting on the couch, no cheap plastic baby toys near her or anywhere in the room. Laurie considers what it would mean for her job if there was no baby. She can't ask to see it for proof. Also, she doesn't like children and shrinks away from their screams.

"Yeah. That's the one," Laurie says as she slips off her shoes and drops her bag by the door. It's quiet except for the gentle tumbling of a dryer behind a heavy door somewhere down the hallway leading to the bedrooms. Laurie licks her lips before she can stop herself. "Would you like to get started right now?"

"Yes. I just want to see if this feels normal, and if it does, we can talk about how often you can come back." The mother has the blonde hair of Laurie's dreams. Thick and long past her shoulders without the halo of split ends common on over-processed heads.

Laurie moves to the couch even though she hasn't yet been prompted to, not really, and she's careful to sit not too close just yet. They'll have to rearrange a few times to get comfortable once the mom's breasts are out and Laurie's smock is on.

"We should get started," the mother says.

"All right." And Laurie gets to work. She stops thinking about the furniture she would carefully carry out of this place wrapped in plastic as if she were just moving down the block to a more spacious loft space with a sunset view of the less spiky side of the city. Instead, she fills her head with the hum of an airplane engine and a mantra of her now-mechanical instructions to herself. The mother doesn't have to ask when to open her shirt. Laurie lets her know it's time by inching closer.

After a few minutes of the regular suction, extraction, and spitting, Laurie feels eyes warming the back of her neck and jerks up to see a human shape disappear behind a wall. "Is someone else here?" she asks the new mom.

"Oh, no. It's just my cleaning lady."

The way she says it makes Laurie consider her own title. Milk lady? She would rather stick with being a humanized breast pump, even if it means she has to admit she's the woman who does the job of a machine.

"I told her you were coming, and she's not supposed to be alarmed. She sometimes makes me move so that I'm not in her way." She pauses to cover her breasts which are lacy with warm green veins. "Ola! Could you come in here a second?"

Ola rounds the corner after Laurie hears her set down an aerosol can on what she imagines is the bathroom counter.

"What's up?" she asks.

"This is Laurie. She works for us now, too." Laurie feels a jolt of success way up in the top part of her spine. Forty dollars a week extra at the very least with the potential for more. The mom turns to Laurie and says, "Ola's Polish, but she speaks English beautifully. It's almost like she was born here."

"Thanks," Ola says, turning away without making eye contact like she's already heard that one before.

"We won't bother you in the living room, right?"

"No, I'll work around you."

Laurie gets back to work but even over the airplane engine hum, she hears the sound of loose plastic vacuum wheels sliding along wood, and she stops her measured extracting, letting milk slowly well up inside of her mouth. She detaches with a small sound and finds the bucket unmoved at her dangling foot.

"Maybe we should move somewhere more private," she asks with an eye on Ola as she enters the room again.

"I'm sorry. It's time for me to vacuum." Ola parks the vacuum on the rug and looks at the canister. "Want me to move that out of the way?"

"I'd rather you not, Ola. It's my milk after all, and you've been cleaning all day. The baby might get sick." The mom picks the canister up and nestles it between her legs so that Laurie will barely have to move to deposit the milk, and Ola will have a clear path vacuuming at their feet. "Whatever you can't get to because of me, I'll understand."

Laurie can see that she might have trouble siphoning from this one, especially if Ola is here every week, sliding in and out of rooms, listening to the splatter of milk echoing off the bare walls. But she manages to finish with the sound of the vacuum drowning out her suctions at least.

"Is it okay?" Laurie asks with Ola straightening stacks of coffee table books on the credenza, her back still turned to a topless mom and Laurie dabbing at the corners of her mouth with a tissue.

"It does save me the trouble of pulling out the machine and washing it and putting it away. You also hurt a little less than the machine. Good job." The mother pats Laurie on the shoulder. It might be a little less confusing than a high five.

"I accept payment by cash or check."

"You'll want the full amount for today?" the mother asks and looks down into her milk pail, appraising the milk level maybe seeing the substance in a new light, like Laurie, measured, bought, and sold by the ounce.

"Yes, I think this has been an hour well spent," Laurie replies with a chuckle. She hears a snort from Ola's direction. After the mom tears a check from her heavy leather-bound book, Laurie slides on her shoes at the same time Ola emerges from the bathroom changed back into her street clothes, a dress Laurie herself would consider buying if she could bear to part with the money resting now at the bottom of her purse. Laurie and Ola leave the apartment together, which is nice because Laurie needs to take a second to explain to Ola what she does. It's not as simple as cleaning a house, and it certainly isn't what it looks like.

CHAPTER FOUR

Ola

"Looks like prostitution to me," Ola says. "But I don't know where the pleasure comes from."

"It's not about pleasure. I'm offering a highly specialized service to people who have the disposable income to give me money."

"So it's a scam."

"It would only be scam if I was depriving these women of something." Laurie winks.

On the walk to the El, Laurie tells Ola a story she's heard from friends all over the states. There are few posted jobs that pay. Everyone is sick of food service, babysitting, and dogwalking. Laurie claims as they stand waiting for a light to change that she created her own demand, her own niche market. Ola has seen those phrases in the how-to articles family members email weekly, imploring her to change her career. It's not a career; it's a gig she tells them.

"Is it a gig or is it a job?" She asks Laurie.

"It could be a career if I can get it to scale well. Just have to figure out a mechanism."

"That's more trouble than it's worth."

After they part, she walks to a bus stop where she'll catch the Damen bus running all the way north to Andersonville, a quiet neighborhood but not much cheaper than where she is right now. As she boards the bus whose doors squeal as they slide closed, she feels a shudder at the thought of holding warm milk in her mouth for too long. She would rather dip her hands in bleach or spritz herself with Pine Sol, a scent that makes her so nauseous she has to make a special request to keep it out of her clients' array of overpriced cleaning products. It is a request that has gotten easier to make after over a year on the job. She knows to assert early what she needs, and that's probably something she and Laurie have in common.

When she gets home, Ola looks around at half of a carefully decorated apartment. All of the big furniture is there, but bare nails stick out from the wall and whole bookshelves are missing their contents. Books, DVDs, and an envelope full of memories in the form of ticket stubs and polaroids fill a box by the door that she needs to complete and send by media mail to Seattle, a city she hopes never to visit. The somebody now living in Seattle has asked to detangle his life from hers after six months apart that were supposed to be just two. The detangling is difficult because there is no ill will between Ola and the somebody else. It's a strategic decision necessitated by something that the somebody else called the "job market." There was mention of a career. There was an insinuation that Ola move. She can clean houses anywhere. Seattle's floors must be difficult to keep clean. Too much mud tracked indoors.

Even though they also live in Chicago, Ola calls her parents instead of visiting. They exchange niceties in Polish, and Ola chooses her words carefully to avoid questions about work or the somebody else, but they come anyway.

"Have you applied for those office jobs Rafał forwarded to you?" her mother asks. They're both on the line with separate headsets probably in two different rooms to avoid that sometimes melodic interference.

"Can I tell you first about the woman I met today? She turns herself into a breast pump for new mothers."

"Did you ask for a business card?" A snide comment from a dad who resents her for not taking a job at the bank with him. She hears the same words and phrases from him, too, on a loop: "not taking advantage of your potential," "college-educated," "ignoring the land of opportunity," "this is not why we came to America."

"Oh, come on. I'm not interested in a job like that." Ola tears paper when she talks on the phone. She's got a stack of confetti growing next to her. She piles nervous habits on to herself, almost by force.

"But you're not interested in anything that pays well. And now that you're alone, you need to think about making a little bit more money to support yourself."

"I'm not alone. I'll find a roommate by next week." The hunt begins that night after three definitive weeks of solitary living. The somebody else is serious about the permanent job he hasn't found yet. She only receives email updates; no phone calls lest she yell.

¢

She saw a car accident when she was twelve. To be fair, she has seen many car accidents, some from the inside of the car involved, but this one was different because of how it unfolded in front of her like a film with missing frames. It was a summer morning. Ola and her brother Rafał were sitting unsupervised on their home's unwelcoming concrete front stoop, which was painted a sick gray at the time. They had played a game which involved jumping down the steps in a particular sequence (1,4,3,2,5), but when they tired of it, they moved to watch stray camp kids in matching t-shirts taking up all four of the baseball diamonds across the street. Their house, second from the corner, also offered a view of the crab apple trees and a stump of a dead one almost three feet wide cut down because of some illness that shriveled even the tips of the thinnest branches stretching up to fifty feet above their heads and clattering in afternoon storms that came on strong from the west.

The street was clear of cars. Most were at work; the backups were tucked safely into garages of the flimsiest plywood and siding construction, but it was nice for Rafał and Ola who needed room to ride their bikes and rollerblades. No one sped in their neighborhood during the day because it was a school zone, and on most days cars floated by with their engine volume turned down so low that they didn't drown out the metal whine of park swings down the block or the quieter plunking of a basketball against the uneven concrete. Their new house (where it was, how much freedom it gave) was a dream for children old enough to go see friends without leaving a very detailed note. The park was a social activity which didn't require planning. Ola could show up and at least one of the neighborhood kids would be there.

The first thing Ola noticed sitting on the steps was the roar she could hear from an engine over a block away. She looked up to see a blur of black and a screech as the car left the street and struck the curb where yesterday Ola had held a hula-hoop contest. The car flipped once onto its roof, and with leftover momentum slid another fifty feet down their road to stop in front of their neighbor Nicole's triangular house. It was a black SUV. It had nearly clipped a woman pushing a stroller near the street corner. No one screamed. Ola doesn't remember the sound of metal on asphalt, which she thinks would have been deafening in the mid-morning slow heat. Before she could react, it happened, like someone had heaped seconds onto each other.

Rafał ran inside for the house phone. Ola went to pound on Nicole's door. Someone called 911. Someone pulled the driver from the car even though he was perfectly fine getting out walking on his own. Someone made tea. And as a group, those home and awake and now shaken sat with the wreckage and him until the ambulance and fire truck came from around behind the high school. Ola was not asked to be a witness. Wasn't that strange? Was she too young or was it clear to the adults in a way that wasn't clear to her what had happened? The seconds had already congealed into a sticky mess.

It's not the car or the loss of control. It's the wordlessness of it.

¢

She returns to her Monday house after a week, knowing she'll have to rush because there's a potential roommate who wants to see the apartment. It's a woman moving from Indiana who says she'll try to beat rush hour traffic but not to count on it. Last week this was where she met Laurie leaning forward like a baby but so much bigger to greedily find nourishment. Not that she really cares what Laurie does to make rent. These are not times to get picky. She won't mind working around Laurie again, but she'll also accept a change in her schedule. Both options are fine by her. She's not inflexible.

When no one answers the buzzer, Ola lets herself in with a key she keeps tucked away in her makeup bag. Before she returns the key to her purse, she pulls out a mirror to make sure her eyebrows are plucked. They are. This woman has commented on her appearance before, suggesting lotions and cleansers and toners, and it's best not to stir up that kind of talk more than once. Familiar and alienating at the same time, Ola doesn't know whether to feel insulted or mothered.

No one is home, so she might be able to get out in three quarters of the time without a mom and a baby to bump into or work around or wait for a nap to be over before she can change the sheets in the crib. She starts in the bedrooms now, stripping sheets to run a wash while she dusts and sweeps the bedrooms. The kitchen gets disinfected from top to bottom, and all the crumbs are swept to the dark slate tile rough with depressions making it hard to clean. The washer buzzes to her that it's finished, and she moves the load into the dryer, pulling the vacuum out of the utility closet since she's right there. Starting in the kitchen, she picks up all the food that has settled in cracks, and then she moves to the piles of dust left in the bedroom doorways, and then she circles around the living room like with a lawnmower, which isn't as efficient as the diagonal back and forth her aunt taught her, but she needs to add some fun sometimes to a routine she can repeat in her sleep. The rug is plush and requires a change in the vacuum's setting. She bends over, exaggerating the feeling of her spine creaking already.

The bathroom is the most difficult because the Jacuzzi tub is surrounded by every type of cosmetic product. All are dusty and unused; most are expired. When she's alone, Ola can first spritz herself or moisturize with something scented organic or manufactured in a high-tech lab. But after preening, she has to move a few bottles at a time to wipe a damp rag spritzed with Lysol on the tile to restore some sparkle. The woman likes it when the bathroom sparkles and all her products are still exactly where she left them. The mirrors take time, too, because there's only one rag that doesn't leave marks or little white fibers stuck to the surface. Ola polishes in circles the way she was taught while looking at herself in the mirror: the wild eyes bloodshot for weeks behind thick glasses, the thin hands with dry skin cracking on the knuckles. But her narrow face is still a perfect oval. She doesn't have any flyaway gray hairs, contrary to what her mom had predicted a few months ago. She makes a note on the inside of her eyelids to look for the liquid band-aid at home. She's afraid it was taken to Seattle, packed by mistake into the wrong toiletries bag.

When the dryer and bathroom are done, Ola does the mop trick and slides a wet rag onto the broom and secures it with a rubber band from her own hair. She dabs a little bit of Murphy Oil Soap onto the wood and spreads it around in a quick even layer. Then, as that dries, she makes the beds and lovingly smooths out the creases as if she's in her own home. It's a cleaning habit Ola can't break, and she laughs at herself every time she smooths and smiles.

When the door clicks open, Ola is just lacing up her tall boots. She watches the wet tires of the stroller leave tracks on the spotless floor.

"I'm taking twenty dollars off your check for a scarf I think you stole," the woman says as she closes the door behind her, inhaling big the fresh powder scent of the candle Ola lit in the bathroom. She drops a purse on a de-cluttered counter and later, Ola knows, will stretch out on a clean bed with her shoes still on. "It's worth a lot more than that, but you've been with the family for a year now, and I know you've been good up until this point."

"I didn't steal from you," Ola says calm. This is not the first time she's been accused of stealing because it's always easier to blame the maid instead of your own absent-mindedness. Never mind that the maid has her own scarves, a drawer full.

"Well, I don't know where this scarf could be. You think it was Laurie?"

"How? You didn't let her out of your sight."

"She's been back here twice since you saw her," she replies without shame.

Ola can't help herself. She starts calculating how much money Laurie can make. Suddenly, she doesn't want to defend her anymore.

Ola leaves in a calculated huff, not angry enough to lose the house but angry enough to show that she wants an apology. After all, she did have to reach over for the diminished check, make eye contact, mumble a thank you, and confirm next week just because that's what she was taught. These people put food on your table, and you don't have a contract, or any legal recourse against them for this kind of mistreatment. Keep your mouth shut and take their money. Those emails from her brother full of new options are starting to look pretty good to her. She might have to take them.

CHAPTER FIVE

Michelle

"It's an IT consulting firm," Michelle says. She is nervous and sitting on a hardback chair, staring across the table at a blonde woman about her age with expertly plucked eyebrows and a half smile on her face. They've already exchanged pleasantries, and now they're on to questions about jobs, a would-be pleasantry if either one had anything to brag about. Michelle doesn't flinch when she finds out Ola is a maid, but she is taken aback by her use of the word. Why not housekeeper? Michelle said she was a server and not a waitress, after all.

"What does an IT consulting firm do?" Ola asks.

"You know," she sighs to gather her thoughts. "It's honestly something I have to research before the interview. I know they just want me for data entry, so I don't have to know anything except for the buzzwords. Figure that in the interview I'll casually say the word 'hardware,' and we'll see where that gets me." Pauses for a laugh she doesn't get. "It's up in Evanston, and this apartment would be great for the commute." Brings it back to the goal of the conversation. When she's not talking, she can hear a clock ticking, but she can't see the clock. To drown out the ticking, she keeps talking. "I'm not even sure how to dress for this interview. Last job I had was at a diner."

"Full disclosure, you're replacing my boyfriend and taking over his so-called office."

"That's okay, I think. As long as your boyfriend doesn't mind?"

"Ex. I should've said ex."

Michelle nods, tries to commiserate, realizes she's only ever lived alone and with parents. Maybe she has saved herself some grief judging by the bitterness in Ola's voice.

"When can you move in?"

"Tonight, really. I mean, I just drove up from Indiana with all of my things, had a temporary place down there in my parents' basement." She think she's gone too far because Ola moves her head a millimeter to the left in a twitch. Michelle knows she's very forward, and she isn't really expecting Ola to say yes, but Ola does, and they carry her stuff up from a clean, white Corolla to a bedroom that will hold little more than a twin bed.

They carry a box of books, a ratty duffel bag stuffed with clothes that are mostly navy and gray, a big plastic bag filled with yarn and shoes, and a heavy, flat bin full of loose papers. She travels light even if it comes at the expense of leaving behind perfectly good furniture half-unpacked in her spacious basement bedroom in addition to some food she knows her parents won't touch: a bag of flaxseed, a jar of coconut oil, and rice noodles.

For tonight, Michelle rolls out a sleeping bag, borrows a towel, and closes the door to her room after writing down the wireless password from underneath the modem. She'll watch Netflix quietly and then prepare for her interview in the morning. Of course, the only thing her father said as she cleared out of the basement she hoped to never return to was, "I can't believe you don't even have work lined up, and to leave your job like that without giving two weeks notice. We won't be able to show our faces there for months, and you know how much your mom loves the fish sticks." Michelle texts him quickly to make sure he knows she's found a place but doesn't expect a response.

¢

She gets the job. Her shirt isn't ironed. Her hair a mess. She almost flubs the question about why she left her last job, but the executive assistant who does the hiring has a soft spot for knitting, and against the advice of career counselors and friends who have Linkedin accounts, Michelle has knitting listed under skills on her resume. It's important, Michelle knows, to make sure that

even hiring managers know you're human. And it's also sometimes important for you and the boss to share an alma mater and
a hometown. She knew there'd be people in Chicago from Portage, but she didn't know that this small, sleek firm was started
by Lucas Goodwyn, her older brother's high school classmate.
Their intertwined history, or the parts of Portage that appear on
her resume are circled in red pen when she looks across to her
interviwer's lap. The talk goes from serious questions to a dis-
cussion of the features on the premier social networking website
for knitters. Dana doesn't like the new search feature, thinks it's
impossible to stumble upon free, nice patterns.

Before Dana tells her about job responsibilities, she introduces her to the entire team (her word, not Michelle's). No one
is more than ten years older than she is, and they have big
smiles set in healthy faces. Michelle is aware of the one crooked
tooth that even braces couldn't budge near the corner of her
own smile. She experimented as a child with smiling sideways,
but instead of drawing attention away from her mouth, she had
concerned teachers asking her daily if maybe her teeth didn't
hurt from some neglected cavity.

She forgets names and knows she'll have trouble differentiat-
ing between Aubrey and Amanda. She'll sit behind one of them,
though, in a private corner of the room with the smaller fax machine. She'll have a phone, but she won't be expected to answer
it unless they're understaffed. The only person in a more remote
location of the office is Mark. He faces a wall, and even when
Dana walks Michelle over for an introduction he continues to
type.

Dana says, smiling, "You and Mark have the same job. Hope-
fully when you take some of the work load off him, he'll relax a
little bit."

Mark takes a break from tabbing through fields of numbers
on a color-coded spreadsheet to half smile at Michelle. "It's mo-
notonous, but you'll get used to it." Curly hair hangs in almost
dirty short tendrils on his forehead. He wears wire-rimmed
glasses with lenses barely bigger than his eyeballs, but he smells

like a sophisticated cologne, certainly something out of a glass bottle.

"You'll start training Michelle when she starts on Wednesday?" Dana asks.

"Sure. It won't take any time at all," he says finally meeting Michelle's eyes. They smile at each other knowing that as long as they're both working here as data enterers, they'll be a unit in the eyes of their office mates.

"I'll show you the rest of the office, Michelle."

The rest of the office turns out to be one more large room with sloping, beautiful wood floors, a bathroom with ornate light fixtures and a room full of immense black filing cabinets where Michelle will spend some of her time filing paper forms and applications.

As they stand around the island of the kitchen, Dana apologizes for how low the hourly wage is, and Michelle holds back a snort of laughter. It is five times more than her pre-tip pay at the diner.

¢

It happens at some point on the red line during her first week of commuting south from Evanston. Michelle is looking at the dour afternoon faces sticking out of trench coats. They all bob with the motion of the train even as their feet remain rooted to the floor. Michelle bobs with them. She imagines walking through the doors with a throng of workers who wouldn't recognize her even if they jostled shoulders every day for a year. They could end up typing on different floors of the same glass building, and she feels anonymous. It's an uncomfortable feeling and it isn't, kind of like toe bones getting rolled between fingers—those little piggies.

She passes her stop without so much as an involuntary jerk in the direction of the clattering doors. Instead, she rides a wave down the entire length of the city. The middle part of Michelle's extended journey takes place underground, while the first third and last third let her see firsthand the difference between the heavily-populated, heaving north side and the dilapidated, cold south side where the defining feature is the Dan Ryan, a congested highway with tall walls, which obscure vacant lots and abandoned storefronts from passing casual travellers. At the final stop on the train, Michelle expects to find herself alone in her compartment, but there are still passengers sharing space with her and lined up to get into the station and back out onto buses heading in every direction. Their journeys don't end here. They end with the whims of the bus drivers who scoot through the city's arteries.

She looks east and finds her view of Indiana obscured by roofs covered in shingles or tar, bricks in the blandest of yellow orange. There isn't much else to expect. A sign with big marquee bulbs pointing the way home? She left enough in Portage—cats that were never hers in the first place, a bed, her 8th grade yearbook, diplomas of all sizes, books—to think of it as home still. She thinks it will take years before she stops pointing north when someone asks her where the lake is.

"Where are you from?" Michelle asks the first person to sit down next to her on the way back home.

"Here. I've lived here all my life," the man says smiling even though he's had to take his headphones out in order to answer this stranger's forward question. He's about Michelle's height but he looks shorter folded into himself to conserve space.

"You don't want to move anywhere else?"

"I got used to it. The weather and all the other problems people complain about. You been here long?" He turns toward Michelle now and straightens up to reveal that his torso is exactly the size she should've expected, given how his legs take up all of the available room between himself at the next row of seats.

"Just a week."

"You'll get used to it, too. And where are you from?"

"Portage, Indiana. Just across the border?" Portage is small, and Michelle doesn't know how to place it for someone who may have never left the state of Illinois, just like her Grandma

Ada never left Indiana after she turned ten.

"I know Portage. You ever get to the beach? At the dunes?"

"From time to time. When I wasn't working."

"Beautiful spots for swimming there." He moves to get up and says, "This is my stop. Good luck." He waves goodbye as the door slides open. He said just enough to be polite, not enough to shed his anonymity. Later in the week, if they happened to be on the same train car, they might not even recognize each other.

¢

At the apartment, Michelle and Ola slide past each other like ghosts, resolving space struggles in front of the bathroom and at the front door with quiet apologies and heads bent to the ground.

"Are you from Chicago originally?" She tries to engage Ola one afternoon when they're both home, which is rare given their irregular hours.

"No. Poland."

"Oh! Is that the language I hear you speaking sometimes on the phone?"

"Yeah."

"I thought maybe it was Russian. Because of your blonde hair, you know."

"Definitely Polish." Ola goes back to typing an email on her laptop, and Michelle stuffs her headphones back into her ears. Their living room is not cramped, which means that Ola commands the large sofa in the center of the room facing the TV, while Michelle sits in a POANG armchair by the bay window, a mason jar of tea on the armrest. She wants full, layered sentences from Ola, but she doesn't know how to punch through with a relevant question that would make her talk as much as she types.

"Also, there are plenty of Polish people with blonde hair," Ola says hardly looking up from her laptop.

The ping of Ola's Facebook guarantees that there's a more active conversation happening somewhere Michelle can't see.

At least Michelle knows without asking that Ola worked today. Her fingers smell like bleach even from across the room.

Another hour passes, and the pings from Ola's laptop are not letting up. Michelle turns her screen so that Ola can't see even a sliver of it, and types in her name on Facebook. She, of course, can't see the chat happening a few feet away from her, and from Ola's frown, Michelle knows it's probably not a fun one. So instead of talking, she scrolls through Ola's profile pictures. They range from silly childhood snapshots of Ola playing in a park, to close-ups of two smiling faces. The face on the left is Ola's, and the one on the right must be the phantom ex. No sign of him in the house except the low box in the hall Michelle keeps tripping over and spilling. She returns to Ola's main profile and clicks add friend, waiting for the hopeful sound from the other side of the room.

When Ola receives the notification, she looks to Michelle and smiles. She clicks accept so that Michelle can sigh in relief.

"Why didn't you just ask me?"

The truth has to do with fear, and she doesn't want Ola to know that. "Element of surprise?" She smiles her crooked smile to reassure.

"Well, here's a surprise back."

Michelle sees her Facebook tab light up with a party invite from Ola to a house in a neighborhood she's never seen. She blindly scrolls through the information, and clicks that she'll be attending before she knows all the details. "Are you sure this is okay with your friend?"

"She's not really a friend, just someone I met once on the bus."

They return to their silence, but the air between them is not so heavy.

She's had moments with Mark. Hasn't told anyone yet. Hasn't had anyone to tell, but there's a spark. He trains her on his computer now, and he types in a work order, and she follows, and the keys he's touched are electric. She drinks gallons of water because everyone else does. Her skin is clear and glowing. She doesn't feel the cling of kitchen grease. Her eyes throb, though, if she glues them too long to one field in their database. Then, it's easy to get codes mixed up resulting in filing nightmares she takes covert hours to detangle in the black room that feels more like the cubicles she expected. Not even Mark comments on her mistakes, and she tries throughout the next few days to fall into trial and error as an efficient method of training. She comes up with easy ways to alphabetize her paper documents as she transfers information from them into the computer so that filing takes half the time it did on her first day. She knows when the mailman comes to drop off a fresh batch of documents for her to unpack and sort. She knows where the bags for the big shredder are. She's still trying to figure out the lunch policy by observing her co-workers' habits.

"How's your first week?" Aubrey or Amanda asks over makeshift lunch. She has stick straight hair down to the middle of her back. Michelle has seen nothing like it, and instinctively reaches for her own fine strands to tie them up into a feather duster of a ponytail. Better to hide it behind her head then let it hang in a bunch at her earlobes, embarrassing around such sleekness.

"Just learning the ropes. Mark is a really good teacher."

"He's been here only about six months. Just took more hours, too. I think he might go full time soon." Aubrey nods approving of the expansion, anticipating a bonus. Lucas sits cooped up in an office that looks more like a play room: glass desk, flat screen TV mounted on the brick, giant monitors for all kinds of spreadsheet work, and windows overlooking the greenery of Northwestern's campus. No one knows how far back their relationship reaches, that she texted her parents right after she was offered the position and asked them if they remembered Lucas Goodwyn, and they responded with a quick note that he had already called to tell them.

And Michelle likes that it's a secret nepotism, and she likes knowing that if an unrelated Mark can be offered a full time position, she might have an even easier time of it. She knows that here "opportunity for advancement" is not just a phrase used to keep hourly employees working toward an invisible goal. There's hope yet that there will be phones to answer and clients to assist, instead of endless forms to process and file. In a few weeks, she'll be leaving all that work to the next Michelle, and she hopes by then to have gotten a handle on her hair so that she can be the encouraging beacon that Aubrey is to her. She hopes she can be responsible for training after Mark's promotion.

CHAPTER SIX

David

David is on what he refers to as the real train that leads to his mother's house in the suburbs. The occasion is a big one so he's wearing clean corduroys and his scuffed brown leather boots. He considered buying flowers but didn't know which ones meant "Welcome back, Grandpa!" so he didn't get any, and sitting on his vinyl seat with lifeless hands, he feels silly. He's now the kind of guy who pays no attention to manners, or his uncombed hair.

His mother lives in an under-populated subdivision plotted for five times more residents, five times more cars on the roads, five times more shoppers in the nearby mall. Giant intersections of roads which once expected commerce change lights from yellow to red to green and back again for multiple cycles without affecting more than a car at a time. David is surprised that Metra maintains their station in such an under-developed spot. Commuters are few and far between. There are even bands of growing corn, unsold land meant for development but still cultivated for marginal profit.

David only visits every two weeks, which Laurie says is too much since everyone involved has lives of their own, and especially since this special family visit is costing him a night at work. But he feels some comfort in the familiarity of stepping off the silver train with unsettling green-tinted windows and into his mother's Honda Odyssey. The car is old enough that it has seen David through much of his childhood including a brief season of soccer and Pokemon cards hidden from his siblings underneath the backseat. And Laurie doesn't understand the benefits of living near family. She left Dubuque at eighteen and has been back a total of four times.

On this windy day, David is about to hop into the passenger seat with his head aimed toward the pavement when he sees his grandpa sitting there, a short leathery man with snow-white nose hair and almost blue eyes. He lifts a hand to greet him, keeping his elbow on the armrest in a motion that looks regal to David. It must be old age that turns every gesture into something meaningful and stately.

In the backseat, David's knees are higher than his hips and his feet are tucked under his mother's seat.

"You have to take me on a day trip to the city, David. I miss it," his grandfather says.

"Of course I will. Maybe tomorrow?" David remembers that the last day they went into the city, they took a pair of old bikes from the garage, stuffed them into the trunk of the Odyssey with the seats removed, and drove to Midway Airport. They parked under the clattering Orange Line and rode their bikes twice around the perimeter of the airport, stopping in the spots where the chain-link fence hadn't been torn down and replaced with solid sheets of steel to block sound and sight. No longer could they feel the heat of the engines singe their faces as the airplanes took off. In those remaining clear spots, though, they watched planes through a thin haze of exhaust, hovering over hot concrete.

"Absolutely not," David's mom interjects. "It's too cold. How about we drive in as a family another day?" She thwarts their plans without turning to look their way even though the car is stopped at an empty intersection, waiting on the sensors to grant a special turn signal.

"But this might be my last chance."

David sighs. His grandpa's favorite topic is mortality. He predicted six months ago that this trip from his modest condo in San Jose, Costa Rica might not happen because he was feeling weaker by the day.

"I know, and then it'll be my fault you didn't get to see Chicago one last time."

"Why did you move all the way out here, Lana? There's not

even a bus."

"There is a bus. You're not allowed to take it, though."

"Why not?"

"Because anywhere you need to go, you can go with me."

David knows this conversation. Not only is it the same one his grandpa has with his mother every visit, but he's asked the same questions, wondering why he was never allowed to take the bus to the mall, or how it came to be that he had to feel like a Chicagoan exiled and in some strange half-hearted sprawl, when he had spent twenty years of his life within the neat grid of the south and north sides.

They pull up to a house with a brick walk, brick doorway, and siding everywhere else that doesn't face the street. Low yellowing grass and manicured evergreen shrubs surround them as they walk to the front door, used only if there are guests. If David's mom had been alone, she would have walked behind the garage to a door leading into the kitchen, where she liked to kick off her shoes and drape a jacket or a sweater over a pine chair set against the wall for getting difficult shoes back on. But they're in the front hall where the décor is austere enough to make David feel like he's ten again and seeing the house for the first time. He pulls three hangers out of the hall closet and hangs up the coats while his grandpa works on untying his shoes.

"Grandpa, I'm sure you don't have to do that."

"I want to. Don't want to be the only person with shoes on in this whole house." He works his heels out slowly from his all-white sneakers. And when he's done, he slides them against the baseboard and keeps close to the wall as he walks to the kitchen.

They've been smoking in there. David can tell right away, given the hazy cloud over the kitchen table.

"Hope we're not eating in here," he says wrinkling his nose.

"Would you rather be driven to a steak house tonight, sir?" his mom asks, mocking him for the apartment that he's splurging on in the city.

His customary seat is empty but there's a pile of Entertainment Weeklys and Sunday Tribunes on the placemat. David's mom knows to save them, and he's got to get through the mound before he leaves tomorrow afternoon. The oldest magazine he flips through just for the pictures since most of the articles strike him as dated: box office predictions for movies already out, baby pictures of some new celebrity he's already seen online, book reviews for the sappy stuff he doesn't have the time for. But the interviews still matter, and he finds himself laughing at some of the snarky remarks directed at some of the worst fall comedies.

"Are we going to talk, or are we going to watch you read?" his mom says as she lights a cigarette and inhales in theatrical exasperation. She should know better than to keep reading material on the kitchen table. For David, reading material can be anything: cereal boxes, month-old community newspapers, and the labels on placemats. All fill his head with an organized chatter.

"Sorry," he says, five years old again. "How was your flight?"

"Long because of that layover in Houston."

"And grandma? She's fine by herself?"

"Oh of course. Gardening and the cats will keep her busy. I'm only gone two weeks though."

"I thought you were staying longer."

"No. Just handling some social security paperwork that I couldn't put off until summer. But maybe you can come back with me."

David wants to say he can't because of a wedding, but he's afraid to tell his mother about the arrangement because if he tells her about the date, she'll assume he was asked while working, and she already said on the phone that his grandfather can't know all of the details. He wants to say that, maybe one day, he'll arrive on the beaches of Costa Rica's Pacific Coast with a wealthy fiancé with curious taste buds and glowing skin that everyone will notice even when she's not undressed for the beach. He'll translate the menus for her and order only the freshest fish.

What comes out of his mouth instead is some bullshit about

how they need him at work because it's a really busy time in late fall as the leaves are turning and people are planning winter weddings.

"Your job sounds very important, David. It's so nice that you're helping people get married," his grandfather says. "You got America all figured out, and all you had to do was go to college and get the education you deserved."

"And take on a bunch of debt I'll be paying off for the next twenty years."

"Maybe you should ask for a raise."

David's mom jumps in. "That's not the way it works, Dad. You know that." When it comes to money talk, she is always quick to disagree with the blind optimism of a man like her father who had moved to this country, became a citizen, and worked a number of jobs (straight, honest jobs he calls them) in order to fund a cushy retirement in Costa Rica. She followed in his footsteps, but ended up in the suburbs with three college-aged children who had sailed on that same wave of blind spirit and ended up in bad shape.

"It does work that way. That's what happened to me. I came and I worked." A predictable statement followed by a smug sip of old coffee. "Heat this up for me, please?"

David grabs the mug and stands to reach the microwave on the counter.

"Can you do it on the stove?"

"In what?"

"Any old pot. Tastes better that way."

At the stove, David looks around for something else to read. There's a pile of old newspaper, and he just wants to see how old the bottom one is, but when he lifts half the stack, he finds a red and white "For Sale By Owner" sign, unmarked still, clearly hidden. He wonders who knows, how much it will embarrass his mother to be confronted in front of her father.

"I don't want it boiling, though. How will I drink it?"

He turns off the gas burner he wishes he had at his apartment, pours the sizzling black coffee back into its mug, and silent on gliding sock feet hands his grandpa the coffee and his mother the "For Sale" sign.

"You're moving?"

She sighs and settles a heavy hand on top of her head as if to bottle in the real explanation. Next to her, David's placid grandfather hides behind his mug, and David knows he knew and understands what the rush was to get into the city. Wherever she's going, this won't be a home base anymore.

"It's not anywhere near here," she says. "I'm moving back to San Jose, but I'm hoping you'll come with me."

"No. I have the Spanish vocabulary of a middle school dropout."

"Oh, your Spanish is beautiful," David's grandpa tries to interject just to say what he says every time David calls Costa Rica and they try the usual exchange in Spanish, hoping it'll sound more interesting then.

"You'd learn." A more honest answer from his mother. "How do you think I learned English?"

"And before then? What would you have me do there?"

"Start work as a translator. You've got a skill. Use it to your advantage. I've got a condo all lined up. Liza and Adam are both going to visit over breaks and said they might come back after school is done. You know Costa Rica's economy is not struggling as bad as this one. I saw it in the paper somewhere." She gets up to rifle through the pile by the stove, and pulls out yellowing newsprint for David to inspect. "It's where I got the idea." She points at a front page photo of three middle-aged women smiling on a couch that looks just like Barb's.

"Why didn't you tell me?" He stares at the almost familiar outline of his mom's home country in the article's graphics. Visits in the past revolved around family. David was carted around from living room to living room for sugary coffee and cookies. He didn't make friends except for distant cousins who laughed at him behind his back for talking a little funny.

"I think your mom wants what's best for you." Another interjection from his grandfather. Another half-truth. But David understands that what they both want from him is immediate agreement. He had no choice but to grow up in this country, and now, they're making him leave it to satisfy themselves, to put all the birds back in their nest.

"Didn't want you to know if the plans fell through." She does have an apology in her eyes. David knows they will hug, and David knows he will make a temporary promise. If he can't find that new job and take the next step, he'll try San Jose. At least he'll be able to run away from his loans. Bank on the government's inability to find him on the western edge of the Caribbean Sea.

He has to ask, "Did you lose your job?"

"No," she says, "But I'm getting old. I don't have health insurance here."

"So you want me to move to Costa Rica because you have cavities?"

"No, I want to move because you might have them. Or does your job dancing around for married women have health benefits?" And because she's his mom saying this, he can't chastise her for revealing his job secret however crudely. Unflinching, his grandfather sips his coffee, still caught in memories of the good old days.

¢

He goes to sleep in his old twin bed after dinner. Under the threadbare Batman sheets, he mostly catches up on his Facebook. Most important is the party he'll have to try and catch tomorrow at Laurie's. It's short notice, but it says she's retiring to make way for a new project, but he wishes that he had better news than a potential move to a country his mom claims has always been a home for him. Every week he sees Laurie, and every week they talk so generically about shaking things up that it makes him more tired than a million bachelorette parties.

It would be easy to quit, and it would be easy to pack up some books and t-shirts into a suitcase and a laptop into a backpack. It would even be easy to leave that basement back in Barb's hands. It would be easiest to leave Club Superior. And it would be difficult to cut his thing with Monica short. His private promise that night has more to do with the prospect of Gold Coast living, of the city's lights winking in the direction of Oprah's penthouses. If Monica offers him the key to that world, he will take it, and he will fix a few cavities, real and imagined.

This string of thoughts, however unreasonable, leads him to a late bout of online shopping. He needs the perfect suit in the most complimentary color. He settles on a light and not quite solid gray to set off his green eyes, which is something someone told him once on a night off, but he won't click buy until he's seen it at the store, and fortunately, he'll have to go back to Chicago to complete that task.

CHAPTER SEVEN

Laurie

At Avalanche & Amble, Laurie drums her fingers on the counter. Joseph is taking his time somewhere in the back. She watches his head move past the porthole window to the kitchen, and even though the window is standard restaurant issue, the door itself is covered in tufted velvet. It was cool when she first saw it. Lately, the décor has felt stuffy, and she wonders why all light and sound from the outside world stop stubbornly at the door. It's smoky, too, even though there's not a cigarette in sight.

"Ah. Here with the delivery? Why don't you take a seat, Alice?" He starts talking before he's through the door, and because he doesn't have any money in his hand and he's not reaching for her jar of milk, she has no choice but to back into a booth.

"I want you to try something new," he continues from behind the bar while gathering ingredients for a drink. He sets a crystal goblet on the counter, pours a precise shot of whiskey into a cocktail shaker along with a little bit of chocolate liqueur. Then, he cracks an egg into a bowl, separates the egg white, letting it bleed through his fingers into a pint glass while the yolk stays intact in his palm, whisks what's in the glass, pauses to dig in a fridge Laurie can't see. He emerges from under the counter with a jar identical to the one she is holding.

"Is that my milk?"

"No. It's probably someone else's. We go through a lot of milk, especially for this drink." He pours the milk into the whisked egg and blends the two until there's a froth. Laurie is already lost in the ingredients. She watches him gather the thick dairy mixture and let it slide into the cocktail shaker where the alcohol is. He shakes with a theatrical flair, smiling in her direction, eventually pouring the beige frothiness into the goblet.

"Impressive," Laurie says.

"Wait until you taste it. We call it 'The Long 19th Century.'" Before he walks the goblet over on a serving tray, Joseph shaves scrolls of dark chocolate onto the drink's surface.

Laurie puts a hand on the base of the goblet to swirl the alcohol and see if she can smell the particular smell of warm baby. She can't no matter how close she puts her nose to it.

"Try it," he says.

She brings the goblet to her lips and takes a small sip of cold froth, and she knows that if she had the ingredients, she would make this drink every night. The chocolate makes it tolerably bitter. "It's delicious," she nods, wiping a mustache of milk off her face.

"I was afraid it would gross you out."

"I deal with milk more than you could ever imagine." She laughs. Hopes that too much wasn't revealed in that comment. "Speaking of which, I've got another twelve ounces for you." It's in playing this role of dealer that Laurie finds comfort. She feels confident reaching for the backpack at her feet, undoing the clasps, extracting a jar of chilly milk, and waiting for the exchange of untraceable and unreportable cash. She wants to concern herself with non-consecutive bills, the results of hard work and weird work and sneaking around.

"Already we're back in business territory," he jokes, drying his palms on the thighs of his jeans. "I'll be back in a minute with your money."

Laurie waits and takes another sip and holds it in her mouth. She watches him through his porthole.

The door to the restaurant doesn't have a bell. It's too classy for that. But it does create a silent suction of air when disturbed. Laurie turns toward the suction she feels to find mom number one walking in, carrying a jar of milk, her coat and purse probably in the car parked illegally in the loading zone out front.

"Laurie! Do you work here?" the mom asks, moving the jar down to her side, not hidden but at least less prominent. "You never told me."

"Flora." Relieved that Joseph took the milk into the back with him, Laurie feels more comfortable lying. "I don't work here. Just stopping in to see a friend." It's an easier lie to continue fabricating. But Laurie wants to ask her former employer about the milk more than anything. It had to be hers still. She's not all dried up. They'll be on an even footing if Laurie gets up now before Joseph comes back. She doesn't want to leave behind the 72 dollars coming her way. She doesn't want to explain herself, cast suspicion on their functional working relationship. There are a million reasons to leave, but they're not tipping the scales. Her one hand is glued to the cold of "The Long 19th Century." She starts counting how many ounces of milk she stole from this mom's referrals.

Skin on Laurie's forehead stretches until it feels like it's cracking. Most of her supply is tainted by Flora's influence. It's not anonymous if two women can sell their wares to the same trendy restaurant downtown. It's not financially viable if all these women are flooding the market with their supply in some kind of rebellious, daredevil move to feel independent from the crying that awaits them at home. What does this woman need seventy two dollars for?

Joseph walks through the porthole door. He and Laurie walk toward each other, and Laurie reaches her hand for the money.

"Thanks for the drink. I really enjoyed it," she says. Quickly, she stuffs the money into her jacket pocket, all crumpled bills. Counting it to make sure it's all there is less important. She wants to get out of there before either one of them opens their mouths with more revealing information. But the scarf and backpack that had been crumpled at her feet are now getting tangled up in her jelly sleeves.

She wiggles and walks, but she's only halfway to the door when Joseph says, "See you later" with a question on his lips.

"Can we talk somewhere private?" the mom asks, glancing over at Laurie.

"Oh, don't worry. You two are moms in the same boat. An

excess of milk, a full baby at home. Or at least I hope you're not starving your babies in order to supply us." He laughs, still not aware of how important Laurie's escape is.

"I'm a mom. She's just a pump," the mom says, slipping into terminology that sounds foreign even to Laurie's ears, even as she spends hours every month tweaking the language of her Craigslist ad, renewing those words every forty eight hours.

"Is her baby dead?" Joseph looks in concern at Laurie who is frozen at the door. Her hand is glued to the handle. The wind is pushing against her through the glass.

"What? No! She never had a baby." The mom turns to look at Laurie, too. "Were you selling him my milk?"

Laurie doesn't answer immediately. She can't run. This woman has her phone number and her legal name, and she has every legal right to report her to some entity. Laurie portrayed her service as something pure and honest, but to be fair, this woman should have understood that losing a client with a little over twelve hours notice put Laurie in an unimaginably tight spot. She needed to make up for the slight and she needed to make up for it quickly.

"I started doing this after you fired me in a text message."

"I didn't have any milk left for you."

"And the jar in your hand? What is it full of?"

"I thought I didn't have any milk left for you."

"You could've called."

"I can deal with one jar of stolen milk, but two is a little much." Joseph interjects in discomfort. Laurie understands that he wants to make a joke of what's unfolding in front of him, but it won't mask the fact that he's involved in something a tiny bit bigger than what he had imagined when dreaming up breast milk delicacies that are admittedly tasty. "Is your milk stolen, Alice?"

"Yes. More or less." Laurie remembers the name she gave herself and turns to see this mom and almost friend narrowing her eyes.

"You're using a fake name, too?"

"Why aren't you?" Laurie shoots back.

"I think it probably goes without saying that this...partnership...is over," Joseph says smiling to Laurie, making light of her loss.

"What if I told you the moms are aware of it."

"I wasn't," the mom says, unhelpful as ever.

"That's because I wasn't stealing from you."

Joseph cuts in, "It doesn't matter, really. I thought you had a baby."

They wait until someone makes a move.

Laurie decides the only way she can save herself is to be the first person out of there, the deliberate actor. She pushes the door open and walks out into blistering wind. Out of necessity and for effect, she walks very close to her enemy's giant SUV to give her a scare. Back through the window, she sees the woman jerk a hand up in surprise and move toward the door. Laurie pretends a friendly wave and looks ahead to the stairs dropping into the tunnel that will lead her home.

The crush of numbers feels like a second coat on her back as she sits sweating on the blue line. She has lost 72 dollars a week, or 288 dollars a month. A very nice chunk of what she owes Mark for rent. He will not hold this loss against her, and that's part of the problem. He wants something better for her, but while she entrepreneurs all over Chicago, he's willing to wait and toil at a job she can hardly describe without yawning. He comes home and keeps her company while she schemes, looks for loans, retail space. A couple months ago, she thought about opening the kind of store she still hasn't worked up the courage to enter. Furniture on white enamel platforms. Track lighting creating tasteful spotlights for her favorite pieces. When she told Mark, he was supportive, but he brought her back down to earth with an immediate Plan B: find a job in retail, move to management, develop a record of increasing sales that might convince a bank you're a good investment. But in many ways, that paperwork and patience felt too difficult and too easy at the same time. It made more sense to save up quick money and muscle her way in. She could be the ultimate success story, pro-filed on blogs all over the world.

At home, that empty dining room/entryway greets her with a whistle from the windows. She forgot to buy plastic for sealing those gaps on her way home. Instead of going back out, Laurie kicks off her shoes and crawls under the covers of their bed. The heft of the comforter, coupled with the newly-installed heat blanket presses comfortably on the length of her body, and it's almost like a hug, and it lulls her to sleep.

When Mark gets home from work, he slips in there with her close enough to touch for the first time in weeks. Laurie hasn't told him yet, but she doesn't want to.

"How was work?" she asks.

"Just the usual. I had a kale smoothie for lunch."

"I think I may have forgotten to eat."

"Let me make you a snack." He rolls off the bed after giving her midsection a quick squeeze.

Laurie waits until she hears the water boiling in the kettle be-fore she gets up to join him. She leans against the doorway, though, not stepping all the way in because if she does, he'll give up the only seat at the peninsula. They used to have two stools, but a leg broke off one of them. Handy Mark had cut short the other two legs to make a seat for the balcony just comfortable enough for a smoke break.

"I had a run-in today."

"With the law?"

"No, maybe worse. The woman who was my first client. Re-member how she basically fired me through text message?"

"Sort of. It's kind of hard to keep track of them."

"She was there at the restaurant, selling her milk."

"I guess she's entitled to do that." His reaction is too small, as if he expects every woman Laurie works for to participate in this black market.

"But if she still had milk, why did she fire me?"

"Maybe it was getting weird."

"Maybe." Laurie watches Mark slice her cheese thin the way

she can't. He arranges it in two tiers on a slice of bread covered in mustard.

"You want some meat on this, too?"

"Sure."

He gets up to dig around in the fridge, pulls out a soggy deli bag and sniffs. And it must be fine because he brings it over to the counter.

"You won't be able to sell milk anymore then."

"No, and I'm worried that I can't extract anymore either." She looks away from his face but not before she catches him smiling at the word. "This is serious, Mark. This woman referred me to all but one of my clients. She's going to call them."

"Then you'll find something else." He shrugs. "You're resourceful."

"Like what?"

"Do what I do. It's boring, but at least I'm not doing anything potentially illegal," he says as he pushes the plate across the counter to her.

"You don't know that." She takes a bite, and even though she prefers warm sandwiches, this one is particularly flavorful with stone ground mustard and ham that ended up not being as mushy as she had expected. Through a mouthful, she says, "Is your company hiring?"

"We were a few weeks ago, but I don't think we are anymore."

"I'd like to have a party."

"For what?"

"I don't know. Maybe I want to celebrate my retirement from the breast milk industry. Call it 'Celebrate My Disappointments!' It's ironic. People will show."

CHAPTER EIGHT

The Party

The party fills out quick even with only a day's notice, and because Laurie and Mark's block is residential, any increase in foot traffic is noted. Three pairs and four lone wolves walk halfway down the block and up the same flight of wooden stairs within an hour. The neighbors notice, but they retreat behind the curtains of modern condos, finish their Sunday dinners, put on the TV, and argue over which shows to watch.

Inside the apartment all available and makeshift seats are snatched and rearranged by friends and friends of friends who want intimate corners in an already intimate space. Laurie has draped lamps with red scarves and pointed most directional lighting at walls and corners away from faces so that everyone looks so healthy, and she supposes some people might be healthier than she is. Some people might still prioritize vegetables over pasta and sleep over streams of information on the internet. But the warm glow of light doesn't erase worry tension from the sides of anyone's face.

She tries to greet each of her guests for a few seconds, avoiding Mark who wasn't ready for a house filled with people even though he knew Laurie was serious about hosting a retirement party. They're both circulating from kitchen to middle room to living room, but he does it in a quiet way, shaking hands and smiling, while Laurie hugs even the newbies, people who are all webbed to her in some way, and she forgets what she had been hoping to celebrate or mourn or whatever the proper term for it is.

Ola stomps through the front door with Michelle. They clear the snow from their boots and look to see a pile of wet shoes by the door. Michelle bends forward to undo the laces on her boots and holds on to Ola's arm while maneuvering her foot out. Thrown off guard by the unexpected contact, Ola wobbles and has to steady herself by grabbing the overloaded coat rack.

The el ride over turned into a tour of the city as Ola knew it. She told Michelle all about her high school haunts: the Dunkin Donuts where she bought salt bagels before they discontinued them at Clark & Lake, the movie theaters clustered together so that you could walk from one to the other to check movie times before smart phones.

"Glad you made it, new friend," Laurie says walking toward the pair. "I'm Laurie," she introduces herself to the other woman. She is shorter and maybe younger than Ola. Her plump cheeks move up to conceal the color of her eyes. Her shoulders are open.

"I'm Michelle," she says, pulling down her hood to reveal clean-smelling brown hair and a wide unlined forehead. "Ola's roommate. Just moved from Portage, Indiana."

"Ola and I work for the same woman," Laurie says.

"You're a housekeeper, too?"

"I wouldn't call her that. But it's up to her to tell you what she really does," Ola says, looking past Laurie to the liquor table pushed up against the windows. She hands Laurie a bottle of wine they both know was on sale at Jewel. She wasn't going to show up to this alone, but Michelle seemed like an easy buffer and maybe a good excuse for leaving early. At their now shared apartment, Ola has heard Michelle go to bed before 11pm, on what they both like to call Portage time, their first shared joke.

"I'm a breast pump. But lately, I've been venturing into marketing bulk breast milk to restaurants for outlandish drinks and dishes," Laurie responds, bottle hanging stiff at her side, a little heavy.

"That sounds really interesting!" Michelle replies. "What are the health benefits of drinking breast milk?"

"I'm gonna go ahead and say that there's probably no difference between breast milk and regular cow's milk. But what do I know? I just sell the stuff." She smiles and hopes that it sounds like the kind of small talk sales pitch she'd like to perfect.

The three stand uncomfortably near the drafty door.

"I think it's better for you," Michelle says eager to please and find new friends. "Cows aren't human after all."

Laurie laughs politely but feels already as if she's neglecting other people who have shown up to see her.

"Anyway, the food is in the kitchen. The drinks are out here. You should let me know if you need anything." Laurie turns to another group and sidles into conversation, speaking as soon as she gets the gist. She's prepared with a YouTube playlist of cute cats on her phone, a snippet of information about Chicago's property values, what's trending on Buzzfeed, and the forever popular question "What is a 401k?"

Michelle wonders if there was something she said to Laurie that made her leave so quickly. The way Laurie hardly exchanged words with Ola makes Michelle feel unwanted, like she's the plus one of the guest everyone was hoping wouldn't show up. Despite the rocky beginning, Michelle wastes no time in introducing herself to the new faces, sidling into conversations that feel open. If there's a triangle of people laughing, she slips in to arrange a square, and before they all quiet down, she says, "I'm Michelle. What are your names?" She holds that it's best to be direct in uncomfortable social situations. And unlike Laurie, her guests are obliging and polite. She meets graduate students and baristas, all making light of their current struggles, although after hearing conversations about books and films and high schools and hometowns, Michelle's not sure struggle is the right word. They have time for leisure even when you wouldn't expect them to. Guilt doesn't affect them in the same way that it jolts her when she thinks about what she's left at home.

"Tell me," she says to a new friend in a cardigan buttoned all the way up and a head band pulling hair away from her clear, round face. "Do you think it's weird that I feel guilty for not being successful?"

"We all imagine different things when we think of success."

Michelle imagines a two-story house with a wrap-around porch and a driveway and time to tend an impressive garden where children watch for prairie dogs and chipmunks dodging in and out of low hedges.

"I saw an interesting quote on Pinterest, probably misattributed but the sentiment was helpful to me. And I don't remember it word for word myself but it was something about how you have to think about success as something that shifts every day. My success was coming out tonight even after I had had a pretty packed day, lots of friends visiting from out of town. On an unsuccessful day, I probably wouldn't have left bed."

Michelle nods and asks, "So it's like a baby steps thing?"

"Yeah, and the opposite of 'keep your eyes on the prize.'"

"What is the prize anyway?"

The two laugh.

¢

Laurie and Mark find themselves two seats on the couch once they hear a steady stream of conversation coming from every room. They don't look at each other, and Laurie doesn't want to explain the scene at the restaurant again, not because he's particularly mean about it, but because she's tired of trying to figure out whether she's supposed to be upset about this or happy enough to be celebrating.

"Are you sure that woman won't report you?" Mark keeps both hands wrapped around his glass. Its plain glass base is no-where near as nice as the cut crystal from a few days ago.

"She ran me off her turf. Reporting me could risk her whole operation."

"You don't have turf. If you had turf, the loss of one restaurant wouldn't necessitate a retirement party." Mark is tired of this affected vocabulary. He doesn't know where Laurie learned it, but it doesn't seem knowing words like "business model," "turf," "return on investment" have done her any good.

"Then what would you call it?"

"I don't know." His knees shake, making the glass in the coffee table dance in its frame. They suspect it's not tempered, given its age. Laurie worries about falling through. Mark doesn't know what he would do with all of that blood. "I'm sorry I ever suggested you sell that milk."

"It's okay. I just have to drop breast milk. There's no money in the easy stuff."

"Maybe you need a good Ponzi scheme." He finally smiles in her direction, but she knows there's an insult right under the surface of that comment. Her work with breasts brought in legitimate money. It bought groceries. It paid rent most of the time. Just because it was a service Mark could never use doesn't mean that it wasn't useful.

The silence between them stretches so long that she doesn't blame him for getting up without a glance in her direction until she sees where he's heading.

"This is a surprise," he says with a smile bigger than Laurie could remember as he walks up to Michelle leaning against the doorframe leading to the kitchen.

"I had no idea I'd find you anywhere outside the office."

"Classic stalker line." Laurie swears Mark is flirting in that innocent boy way. And her suspicions are confirmed when Michelle laughs at his weak joke. Maybe Mark had invited her to the party. Maybe arriving with Ola was a clever way to mask a budding relationship. Workplace romance is what articles on infidelity call it, as if it were a special type.

She wants Mark to feel guilt for a change, so she catalogues the transgressions to bring up later in a bed she doesn't want to stop sharing. Mark didn't tell her there was a new girl at work; Mark interrupted their conversation to talk to someone else; Mark made a flirty joke; Mark didn't want to help her devise a new plan; Mark would be happier with someone like Michelle in all her clean innocence with the baby smell coming off her skin and not her mouth; Michelle took a job Laurie could've had at the office.

David needs to see this, she thinks, but he is late because of the Metra. He would be able to read Mark's advances and tell her that there's nothing to worry about. He would suggest a common sense conversation later after all the guests have left where Laurie admits she's hurt, explains her feelings, and takes care not to read anything on to Mark until he is able to speak for himself. David is good at talking her down. But because he isn't there, she stews on the couch and watches Mark narrate some workplace dramas and offer tips for Michelle's survival in the world of smoothies and mud mask facials.

David texts: "I'm on the blue line."

Laurie replies: "Good. I've got a situation." She knows he won't receive it until he's out of the tunnels, but she wants him to hurry. While she waits, there are dishes to do so that the sink doesn't overflow, and she has to find more wine in the closet stash since nearly every bottle is empty. The party feels small because there's a contingent of chain smokers out on the deck, and the rest take up less space sitting on the floor by the windows than they would standing in the middle of each room with straight backs and wide stances.

Mark spots Laurie looking at him from where they were sitting on the couch. She's frowning in his direction, and then at her phone, and then back up where she sees Michelle and the friend she mentioned getting ready to leave. But before Mark can go say his goodbyes, Laurie lifts herself up from the sagging couch and cuts the pair off before they can turn the doorknob.

"You're heading out already?" she asks Ola and Michelle when she catches them by the door again.

"Yeah, it's a long train ride back to Andersonville," Michelle says. Her hair is longer than Laurie's, and it's cut bluntly to make her face look rounder, younger.

"Fancy neighborhood," Laurie says, taking what looks to be a kind of fighting stance, probably overkill.

"Not any fancier than this one," Ola says. Laurie inhales to reply, but Ola cuts her off. "I don't need someone who just

moved to Logan Square after college telling me where I'm allowed to live. Gentrification is gentrification."

"I'm just saying I don't think I could afford your rent." Laurie
backs away with her hands up in exaggerated defense. And she's
half right. An apartment their size would cost a fortune in Andersonville. And Mark offered to pay the difference when they
were looking at places, seeing as it would have cut his commute
in half, but Laurie even then when she didn't have any idea of
what would happen next was adamant about splitting everything
down the middle.

"You'd be surprised," Ola mumbles as she struggles with her
coat zipper, shakes her head, wonders why she came if the only
other interaction she had with Laurie was an almost fight. Laurie
is intriguing but unpleasant, focused on getting people to think
her way even when there's nothing at stake.

"I didn't come by to insult your neighborhood. Just wanted
to invite you two over some time next week."

"Maybe another party?" Michelle asks, eager to return and
spend some legitimate time with Mark outside of work.

"We do this pretty often, Mark and I." They do. It's not a lie,
but she's glad nevertheless that Mark isn't there to hear her
spinning something of a web for reasons that haven't quite co-
agulated into a plan yet.

"Send us more info. You clearly know where to find us," Ola
says in that way that is both insulting and matter-of-fact.

Laurie doesn't stop them from leaving and kicks herself for
not doing it when David walks through the door minutes later.
They hug as friends do, but she holds on a little longer, hoping
Mark sees, and he doesn't. But she does enjoy the warmth of another person and realizes that her hands are always colder than
the breasts she touches. She can't explain to David how the conversation between Michelle and Mark went. She can't remember
the jokes or the tone of their laughter. David has no choice but
to tell her it was probably nothing. He reminds her of the relationship that the two of them share, its unremarkable platonic-
ness and how often they're mistaken for "lovers."

"Would you be willing to help me out with a new venture?" Laurie asks after she realizes that she can't explain the almost infidelity she witnessed.

"What? No more milking?"

"Did you even read the Facebook event?"

"Thought it was a stunt to get more people to show up."

Like all of her plans, she convinces herself it came to her in an isolated thought package, unrelated to her experiences, research, or fears. She thinks of David living alone in a basement, of Ola losing someone so important to her to the job market, of Michelle here in a new city, and sees their loneliness as something she might be able to solve, and kill two birds with one stone. Now she knows that she won't accept Mark's advice anymore when he counsels her, which means it doesn't matter what he had to say about her future plans. She'll plow ahead. David will help her without question. He wants money, and by next week, he'll have already been a wedding escort. Katie and Tina won't do it because they're both education majors still hoping to find teaching positions. They are careful to avoid finding their way into compromising situations. Even now, they hold small mugs of wine away from their faces. Ola, too, could be convinced with the promise of cash, and Laurie thinks there is little difference between doing someone's laundry and getting into bed with them. James would be an asset to help her figure out a pricing system, but he's on the cusp of being engaged. But Michelle, the newcomer, might be an easy target. Moving costs money, and Laurie knows that she doesn't make all that much money working fifteen hours a week at the office. That way, Laurie could keep tabs on her, let it be known that she and Mark are a unit.

¢

"I need you for something kind of seedy." It's best to lay it all out on the table early, admit that the only good ways to make money are the dangerous ones.

"I will not sell drugs."

"Will you cuddle for cash?"

"No."

"Just once to see how it feels?"

"No."

"You're single."

"I am."

"So what's the big deal?"

"What kind of a creep would want a stranger to cuddle them?"

"I don't know. Haven't done the market research yet." Couching it in economic terms seems natural enough. She's interested in cuddling as a business, but in order to profit from it, she does need to know what kind of loneliness would lead someone to call or email requesting a companion for something so innocent.

"I'm not going to just say yes to any hare-brained scheme of yours."

"Can you try it once and tell me what you think?"

"No."

"I'll let you know when I've figured out some more of this stuff." Laurie needs support on this. She went into breast pumping alone with Mark agreeing only after she convinced him that they could have all of the things they wanted straight out of college (cable, bar crawls, date nights). She knows David misses the relative luxury of dorm rooms and dining halls. "But I can promise you that the extra money will make your heating bill a little easier to deal with this month."

He shakes his head and says, "I need to see where this Monica date takes me first."

Laurie takes a break and moves to put some soft folk music on. Her way of winding a party down, indicating to everyone that soon it'll be bedtime. This process isn't an invasive one, and even though it takes over an hour for the remaining guests to head out with only David left chatting with Mark on the couch where she left him, no one feels slighted or embarrassed for overstaying a welcome.

David stays on the couch because he says he's not in the mood to see frail Barb standing in the window, never sleeping, always spying on his comings and goings.

"She cares about you," Mark says, as he gets up, stretches his arms out and then into a few circles. "Goodnight, guys."

"I might have to move to Costa Rica," David says when they're finally alone. "My mom has made almost all of the arrangements." Laurie is the first person he's telling, and when he says it, he realizes just how scared he is of having to sell or pack up an apartment's worth of accumulated life, the kinds of objects that are just stuff until you have to get rid of them. His mattress, the one he was preserving for a better time, will go to someone who couldn't care less about it as a sound investment.

"You won't have to go anywhere if I can get this cuddling thing off the ground. I'll move you straight into management."

"I'd rather just marry rich."

"What if you don't like the woman?"

"It doesn't matter what I do and do not like. I'm thinking of the future." David wonders if that's even true, imagines Monica's life as a life of total freedom, his as a life of dependence regardless of whether or not he finds that dream bride. But he'd rather be dependent on someone other than his mom for a change.

CHAPTER NINE

Ola

Ola keeps Gmail open whenever she is on her laptop. It's an instinct now to have multiple tabs open so that notifications are instantaneous, even when there's no news to expect. She's making herself available to news. She downloads productivity software that blocks all of her fun sites and immediately deletes it because the internet should be free. She shouldn't have to artificially block bits of it in order to get work done. What work anyway? Ola has been out of college for two years. She writes poetry from time to time but only when she's angry, which is more often than not since the separation. She reads ebooks and plays Tetris so hard that her fingers cramp up. Artificial coffee shop sounds coming tinny through the speakers keep her feeling like she's productive, using apps proven to make her get things done.

Dear Ola,

I need that stuff I left in the apartment. Still don't have a job, or a paying one at least. The internship is good. I'm doing more than just making copies, just so you know. The staff rely on my ideas at meetings, and in the past few weeks, I've been able to sit around the conference table. They want to pay me, but we're working on this new app, and all the ad revenue is tied up in development. I'm pretty good at coming up with ideas, but I don't know all that much about the actual making of apps. I'm taking a class, though. Seattle is crawling with all of that tech stuff. It feels like this is where I belong, and I think I'm gonna stay here as long as I can. How are you? I texted your brother, but he didn't offer up very much information. I know you're alive because I see your green dot pop up every now and then on Gmail. Wish you were here with me. I live closer to the water than even where we lived in Chicago (and I guess you still live there). As soon as I get a job, I want to start paying you rent again. I know you're stuck there for six more months. Maybe you can come out here after the lease is up. Anyway, I want to talk to you. My number hasn't changed.

> *Love,*
> *Alex*

And then a text message: "I sent you an email. Please respond."

She texts back: "I'll get to it soon." But he knows already that her green dot on Gmail has read the email more than once. And he's reminding her that he's a green dot on there, too. They could just g-chat or hangout or whatever it's called this week. And they could text at the same time while she's composing an email response. Three channels of communication open and brimming with expectant static and the distant echo of plastic keyboard keys floating over some green motherboard.

She distracts herself with Craigslist, compares her weekly income with what she could possibly make as the kind of bit translator her parents make her out to be to their friends. Listings stream in, mostly spam. The same listing for a personal assistant with model looks, three times posted in unrelated job categories. Mostly, she hangs out in the gigs section because that's where people try to get labor for free, and there's nothing more anger-inducing than people who seem like they could pay for a service trying to get it for free. Artists need models for sketch classes. Writers need editors for their self-published works of cultural criticism. All of those gigs used to pay, or that's the feeling she has about the years before she got out of college, but that might be a myth or at the very least some kind of story circulating among the people she knows so that they can maintain their helplessness. At least Laurie is trying to move away from the permanent griping she sees on the internet by actively seeking out new venues for all of her odd services.

Michelle interrupts Ola's thinking with so much noise in the kitchen. Their cabinets overflow with pots and pans, and Michelle insists on cooking her pasta in the mid-sized pot, which is in the middle of the precarious stack. It's a motion Alex was able to accomplish quietly even in the early mornings when she was so easy to wake and he was up with an inexplicable insomnia.

Hi Alex,

Don't worry about rent. I've found someone to fill the office space. She doesn't take up a lot of room, but she does make a lot of noise. Good to hear that you're doing well at work. You know, though, that I'm not ready to move away from the city. Will try to visit if I can scrape some money together. There are some friends I'd like to see out there anyway. I promise I'll send the box this week. I'm sorry about the hold up.

Ola

He'll expect more, and she might get a text in a matter of minutes asking for elaboration, criticizing her friendly-yet-distant tone. His Gmail avatar is green again. She can imagine him reading in a café with a coffee on the left side of the table, ready to type a furious response about how he didn't mean to make it look like he was putting an almost career before a stable relationship. All he wanted was her in Seattle where they could own the city as young professionals in sleek trench coats.

¢

The next day, Ola takes a stab at young professionalism herself in the form of a long overdue interview at an insurance office. Her parents had told her over the phone that it was important for her to be prepared for anything including translation tests, a mock interaction with an unruly and impatient customer, history tests, questions about how many years she had spent whole Saturdays in Polish school, and the regular questions about her ambitions and goals.

The office is nestled into a strip mall out in the suburbs, and while it made sense for Ola to take the bus just this once, she'll do what she can to wrangle a car from her parents who no longer need three with only two people left in the house. Her first choice would have to be the 1995 cream yellow Volvo 850. She has only a few years left before driving the station wagon goes from being ironic to sad. Bill, the man and family friend who will be interviewing her, drives a BMW convertible with bald tires. When she was younger, Ola would go for spins around the block with Bill. Her upper body hung over the side of the door like a dog's, her hair a column above her head.

She's sick of listening to the sound of the bus's engine working itself into a sweat when it pulls away from every intersection. The back of the bus where Ola sits out of high school habit vibrates with the effort of pushing all of this clunky weight. All buses look so bottom-heavy and stiff, she thinks, and pretty unlikely to tip over even on a sharp turn.

Inside, the office smells like a shredder when the engine is overworked. The coffee pot hisses and gurgles loud enough for the whole office to hear, which isn't saying much since there are eight desks arranged around a modest room, and only two of them look like they might be occupied. The desk closest to the door has a small computer at the far end, and it's covered in post-it notes. Blue, pink, yellow, and orange squares of paper note important dates, policy numbers, "don't forget the milk"s, cryptic half-addresses, and particularly elaborate doodles. Stuck to the writing surface of the desk are post-its as comic strips. In the panels, a woman with huge curly hair sits behind a plain desk and says things like, "No, thank you, sir, for that invigorating conference call." She never interacts with other characters face-to-face.

"This person is a pretty talented artist," Ola says since she can't avoid admitting that she's been staring instead of following

Bill into the conference room at the back.

"Corinne draws when she's done with all of her work, which should be never considering she's full time, but she's the most competent insurance agent I've ever seen. Been trying to catch her making a mistake for weeks now."

"Are the other employees creative types?"

"Depends on what you mean. Everyone has to have a hobby."

"I don't really."

"What do you do after work?"

"I research cars, I read."

"Well there you go."

Bill ushers Ola into a conference room with no windows and bare walls. A tray of stale cookies sits in the middle of the table.

"Help yourself," Bill gestures, and Ola leans far to pick up two cookies.

"So how did you finally decide to apply for the position? I know your parents have been hounding you for ages," Bill says after a pause in which he rearranges his hands on his wide belly.

"I can be fairly competitive, and I want to get a job here before my ex does in Seattle." What Ola thinks that translates to is go-getterness.

"What happens if this ex in Seattle gets a better job?"

"He'll win and then I'll be the fool."

"But would you stay?"

"Oh, yes. I'm very dependable and all the other stuff it says on my resume."

Bill looks down and scans, moving his thumb down the left edge of the crowded sheet of paper.

"It looks like your most recent position as a 'Home Hygiene Technician' is your most steady employment, a year and a half."

"That's right."

"What did that position entail?"

"I'm sure my parents already told you that I clean houses."

Bills clears his throat, "Is it hard work?"

"Yeah, but it lacks prestige." The second half of that sentence hangs between them. Prestige is not a word uttered in relation to this job either. Business casual is a step in the right direction, but it's certainly not the peak of respectability.

"Well, you know this job requires a different set of skills."

Ola nods. Looks like the person they have cleaning the office already does a decent job. It's difficult to wash the dinginess out of linoleum.

"How about a Polish test then?"

"Oh, come on, Bill. You've seen me speaking Polish since I was a kid."

"I know, but it's just a formality."

"Jakie słowa byś chciał usłyszeć?"

"What does that mean?" he asks, eager to learn.

"I asked which words you would like to hear?"

"Credit card."

"Karta kredytowa."

"Receipt."

"Rachunek."

"Red shoe."

"Czerwony but."

"Insurance."

"Ubezpieczenie."

"Payment?"

"Opłata."

"Pig."

She hesitates. This is what she was afraid of, translating words for potential insults, but she has no choice. "Świnia."

"Cow?"

"Krowa."

"Car."

"Samochód or auto."

"What's the difference?"

"One comes from automobile, the other one describes a car as something that moves on its own without a human propelling it."

"I only ever remember how to swear in Polish."

"I understand why you need me then."

"You know that insurance is not for the squeamish. People will never come to you with happy stories."

"I know."

"You will have to translate their sadness."

Ola pauses before she says, "I know."

¢

Dear Alex,

I have a job in reception at a new insurance firm. It's only two days a week, but I think that with the extra income there, I might be able to come and visit in a month or two. Hope you're doing well.

Ola

She keeps it short in the hopes that Alex won't think she's just rubbing it in. Or is it supposed to be the opposite? Maybe she'll write more after she receives confirmation from Bill that she does have the job. In the meantime, she'll shuffle her schedule around.

¢

At the scarf house, she expects to find an empty house like last week, but instead runs into Laurie doing the work she said she was giving up. The women pause the extraction to say hello to Ola. The mother asks Ola to start her work in the bathrooms this week. Ola obliges, removes her boots and puts on her house cleaning sneakers. She grumbles under her breath, thinks snide things about the woman who just two weeks ago accused her of something she hadn't done. She has at least twenty scarves for all four seasons in colorful prints and dark, nubby wools. She does not want this woman's scarves.

What she does want to do is get out of here after doing the bare minimum. She starts by scrubbing soap scum and gathering stray hairs into corners for easy pickup with a rag. Bath mats get piled into the hallway for their monthly wash. If she wasn't taking out her frustrations on the house, or if this were her sprawling condo, Ola might consider doing a deep clean of the grout. It's starting to look a little gray, but until Louisa tells her to do it, and offers to tack on some extra cash for it, she'll feign blindness.

Ola is in the kitchen by the time Laurie finishes up, dabbing at the corners of her mouth with a tissue.

"Do you want to come over later? Did you get my friend request and message? I've got a business opportunity I don't think you should pass up," Laurie asks Ola. She is almost breathless with her hard sell.

Ola is about to open her mouth to say no, she's found a new job, but before she can formulate the thought, their employer jumps in.

"You're not trying to take Ola away from me, are you?" Louisa asks. "She'll be difficult to replace. Not many cleaning ladies are so young and quick."

"I don't want to steal Ola. I'm just considering a new business venture, and I'd like her input."

"Well, I hope this cryptic business venture doesn't affect both of your abilities to come here."

"Don't worry. As long as there's milk in those mammary glands. I'll be here."

"And you Ola?"

What was she supposed to say in response? As long as you continue sweating dark stains into your white sheets, as long as you leave food scraps in your sink, as long as you track mud into your hallway without wiping it up, I'll be here. She can't bring herself to do it so she stays silent and resumes the task of eliminating streaks on the face of the stainless steel fridge. Phantom dust tickles her nose. She starts sweating into the rubber gloves protecting her skin. The streaks are stubborn and imperceptible to anyone but Louisa. There is a price to pay for stainless steel. Just like there's a price to pay for floor to ceiling windows or good china and it's a cost that is too quickly passed off to Ola—

the maintainer of what is high maintenance, the Spring cleaner, the person you pay to feel guilty about your junk drawer and its disarray.

"She's not stealing me. I'm quitting. Effective now." This is the moment to throw the rag on the floor and spit on it, but that's the kind of moment she won't allow herself. Then, the gig becomes more than what it is, turns into a career or something that shapes her daily behavior in a permanent way. She just came in once a week and cleaned. No hard feelings. She'll find another gig, another house. Or she'll transition into insurance where the pay is worse, but her clients might respect the service she offers, even if they hate insurance just as much as they hate dust.

"But be reasonable, Ola."

"Don't worry. You'll find more than one person willing to do this, and while you look, you can just ask Laurie to pull double duty."

Louisa turns to look at Laurie and says, "No offense, Laurie, but you're here to do only one thing."

"Don't worry. I'm not really interested in doing your laundry. I've got a lot of other projects on my back burner, too."

The two women walk downstairs together after being paid in silence by Louisa, and Laurie congratulates Ola on quitting. "Why so abrupt, though?"

"This woman accused me of stealing her scarf, docked my pay. I'm sick of that kind of shit happening to me," Ola replies.

"Does it happen often?"

"I'm surprised it doesn't happen to you." Neither Ola nor Laurie have any legal protection when it comes to their jobs. Ola thought that meant they'd be on a more even footing.

"Now that you're down some cash, maybe you'll be more interested in my proposition?"

"I got another job. I told you."

"You too?" Laurie asks, and Ola can sense a dejection in her tone that she hasn't heard before. In her eyes, Laurie fails because she tries too hard to succeed too big. She'd move across the country if she heard there was a baby boom in a city she had never laid eyes on. She'd step lightly on the thread separating the legal from the slightly illegal just to prove that new was necessary because nobody cared about old. And Ola felt old already. The cleaning that made her bones ache, the office job that knew no decade, the boyfriend who moved for work settled in so comfortable to their relationship that he assumed she'd follow wherever.

CHAPTER TEN

David

The club is set back from the street and shielded by a seven-foot tall hedge. The leaves are green with bright red tips. David holds the gray of his sleeve up to them to imagine how it'll photograph, and the arrangement of all three colors pleases him in a way that black wouldn't have. He did not want to look like a waiter at a really early holiday party.

A man sitting in a booth by the gate waves him through while mouthing the word "wedding." He doesn't bother to ask for an invitation like he's supposed to, which to David is like passing the first test. He looks like a man attending a wedding at a yacht club, or it could just be the small gift he's holding. Inside of the cardboard box he wrapped in lace print blue paper are two mugs (Mr. and Mrs. printed on the clean ceramic) and a tea infuser. He chose the gift mostly for its size. If the bride and groom don't like it, they'll be able to hide it deep in some cabinet of an oversized kitchen before they donate it to the Salvation Army, where a college student might pick the set up to start furnishing a dorm kitchenette. Plus, his mom says that money at weddings is scrutinized too closely, and he'd rather have a forgettable gift than one that requires any kind of consideration.

He pulls out his cellphone and texts Monica. He imagines her wristlet buzzing on a table while she sips a quiet champagne during the pre-ceremony cocktail hour—or maybe that's not allowed. Maybe champagne is only allowed at the toast. Would Wikipedia know? He decides not to check, it'll just look to the security guy like he's not excited to go in. So he pushes open the heavy cedar door and finds himself in a large hall that overlooks Lake Michigan with Navy Pier an almost hazy strip to the north and a blue expanse stretching and shimmering flat to the east and south. It's striking framed by the dark wood of the club-house. Classic wooden chairs—far fewer than David had imagined—are arranged in two clusters facing the water and an arch covered in cascading hydrangeas. It's a poster wedding, a catalog wedding, nothing like a wedding he would imagine for himself or for his friends, and it hasn't even started yet.

"David!" He hears his name called, and before he turns around, he knows Monica is walking toward him. "Just saw your text. I was just grabbing you a drink. Hope you like grapefruit juice."

"What is it?" He asks, taking a tall, simple glass from her hand.

"A Salty Dog. Alli and Blake's signature drink. Mine's a Grey-hound because I get a little bloated after too much salt." She holds the straw in her hand. The wristlet David was imagining is not a wristlet after all but a quilted leather purse on the longest and most delicate gold chain clinging to her bare shoulder. A lavender halter dress swirls around the back of her neck, and the way it gets narrow at the top accentuates how it gets bigger in the hips and stops just before her rocky knees. He doesn't know much about dresses, and he knows that bridesmaids dresses are supposed to be bad, so maybe this one is too. But the color is nice, subtle, and he likes her arms, taut from the early morning workouts he imagines for her.

"You look very nice," he says. "Hey, where should I put this present?"

"That's sweet of you. We'll take it over to the gift table at the back here. Someone from the club will handle the packaging and transport. I arranged it weeks ago."

Each one of her sentences has David asking himself ques-tions. Was it sweet of him to complement the dress? Or was it sweet of him to bring the gift? Was he not supposed to bring the gift? Is this not really a date? Are they not opening gifts here? Should he have held on to it through the ceremony? Will the packaged gifts be packaged again? When he speaks again, he set-tles on the innocuous.

"Was it a tough job to be maid of honor for such a big wedding?"

"My job isn't over yet." She takes the gift from his hand, shakes it near her ear hard enough to disturb her teardrop earrings, hears nothing, sets it down on the table watched by a man even younger than David in a burgundy vest and a white shirt with too-long sleeves. "Thanks for taking care of all these presents," she says to the boy. And when she turns to face David again, she sees something over his shoulder. David turns to follow her gaze. In the foreground is a short man in a tight suit near bursting to cover his barrel chest.

"Ah! So here's the mysterious David," the man says in a low voice that reverberates in David's chest even during the pauses between words. He pronounces his name the way only his mom does. The i replaced with a long e. "Tell me, how many of these have you done?"

"A few. The older I get, the more weddings I get to witness."

The man looks at Monica, gives her a wink. He says, "My name's Andrew."

"Hi Andrew. I'd introduce myself, but you already know who I am," David says with a smile and grabs Andrew's hand into a solid, practiced handshake.

"Hope you know how to dance, David. Gotta go grab me a drink before the bar closes." And with that Andrew turns away.

They sit down before Monica has a chance to introduce him to anyone else, and within thirty seconds a light bell rings. Monica jumps to her feet and says it's time for her to go be a bridesmaid. All the chairs around David are still empty, and he realizes how lucky it is that he has sat down early. Now, people will have to come to him. He tries to catch Andrew's eye, but the man has settled into an aisle seat three rows from the front where he'll presumably be able to see all of the action without being blocked by one of the burly football player types that seem to make up a lot of this guest list.

It's not that David doesn't like weddings. The ones he told Andrew he got to witness were actually witnessed on Facebook where he scrolled through hundreds of photos of farmhouse and banquet hall weddings, each one depressing in how generic it looked from the outside. Speeches, playlists, arguments were never preserved so thoroughly as mason jar centerpieces. He doesn't like standing by watching other people have fun, or what looks like fun when they smile for a conveniently placed camera. This is his first wedding that isn't family. And he's happy to get his toes wet in a setting where barely anyone knows his name. He can sit back and watch, judging the construction with an eagle eye, editing the fantasy he hadn't known had taken full shape in his mind.

Part of what he used to worry about in weddings was the fake religiosity. This couple, the bride whom he only knows in passing as a client who wasn't very good at Scrabble, and the groom, who may or may not be a pretty prominent football player on the Bears are going to stand before god and anyone else willing to look on. When he could watch others from a distance he wondered why god only appeared for these people when things were really good or really bad but never in between? He wanted to know from everyone who used god so sparingly how they would rank their own belief on a scale of one to ten. He imagined a blog series in which he would interview ten different people who claim to have ten different levels of belief. David thought he could maybe be a five. He doesn't know where the bride and groom fall on this scale yet, but now that he's here, it matters less. What he's worried about now is making an impression here in order to make sure that he can have this in the near future.

¢

He is ready to cry during the procession. He's ready to share some happiness. She's beautiful in a strapless ball gown laced with gold along the edges. And it's all just so sumptuous, like David could fall into her skirts as if they were a pile of pillows. Groomsmen and groom stand in a line smiling and ribbing each other playfully. Everyone is smiling and laughing and there are tears rolling down Monica's cheeks because this is her show. All of the purples of the dresses are working against the blinding gold of the accents and the white of the flowers. She's glowing for the bride, and David is feeling himself grow warm for Monica. She planned this. She made the colors play so beautifully against each other. Of course, maybe even David could do this with the right kind of budget. And if there's one thing that he should be able to tell about this wedding is that it did have the right kind of budget.

The vows are touching, filled with small glances and smiles. David will not remember even a word to report to Laurie. He listens to the sniffles coming from the crowd like bird chirps orchestrated to call one after another in song. He smiles and claps politely after the couple kiss and the photographers have had their fill of kissing shots. He could've cried here too if it wasn't for the fact that now was really the time to focus and re-double his efforts. He can't get Monica alone for very long tonight. He knows that, but he needs to plant the seed, suggest perhaps that he would plan the nicest date for the two of them. What that date might look like, he's not yet sure. Monica has probably done the strolls down the lakefront, the museums, tiny restaurants with fixed menus, the symphony orchestra.

¢

On their way to the cultural center, the core group winds through Millennium Park with two photographers at their heels. David wasn't technically supposed to be there, but Monica made him promise to hang back during the official photography, and they'd still have a little bit of time to walk quietly by themselves. Tourists and weekend park goers enjoying the last warm days of the season stop to stare at the traveling party. David imagines the wedding of Kitty and Levin in *Anna Karenina* and knows that under normal circumstances, he'd be the one staring through the church windows at opulence. Furthermore, this opulence is met with a dose of scorn and not the celebration Tolstoy imagined. Those strolling in the park stopped by a wedding party posing for a photo in front of native prairie grass shake their heads as they try to find a long way around and laugh at the women in high heels stumbling over the fine gravel almost like sand. People are looking at him in the same way he looks at the covers of *People* and *Us Weekly* as he stands in line to buy his groceries. He feels conspicuous for the first time since he prepared to confront the man at the gate of the yacht club.

On the snaking bridge over Congress Ave, he kisses Monica on the cheek with both cameras pointed at him. She puts on a delighted face and holds her smiling mouth open for just a second after he has already unglued himself.

"Thanks, David! I bet that one will turn out great!" she says, and even though he is still thinking about how soft the skin of her face was, he follows her when she rises from the bench to find the rest of the party.

By the time he gets to the green grass in front of the band shell, they're all doing the jumping photos. Instead of participating, David hangs back to playfully point out the one person who invariably stays rooted to the ground at the exact wrong moment. He tries to remember the guy's name, thinks it might be Pat, and makes a note that he can now make some small talk with him later at the reception. The ceremony was great because all attention was focused on the couple. He could pretend himself to be one of their dear friends, smiling at the inside jokes in the vows, an expression of fondness on his face, shining eyes pointed at Monica who didn't see him wipe a tear from the inner corner of his eye.

¢

He forgets how beautiful the cultural center is in between his rare visits. The busy lobby hasn't changed since the first time he saw it as a boy, led to a small round table by his grandpa to hear high school poets tell stories about their neighborhoods, most of which he hadn't seen yet. They split a bag of pretzels and watched ten kids not much older than he was at the time stand in front of the microphone, bump their teeth on its cold metal surface, smile in embarrassment and tell the unlikely mix of tourists and locals about their schools, their homes, their playgrounds. He wanted to publicly proclaim allegiance to something then, too, but wasn't sure to what or how. Nevertheless, his grandfather leaned over and whispered in his ear, "That could be you one day."

Upstairs, the largest Tiffany glass dome in the world centers the sprawling reception space. In today's light the dome is a beautiful blue-green. Surrounding it is an intricate floral design stretching down to the arches and columns that divide the space. No surface is unembellished, and he feels like he's in a garden trapped in mosaic. The dance floor in the middle is flanked by two groupings of round tables with tall gold chairs that would look disproportionate and rickety if not for their gleaming uniformity. White table cloths provide an unfussy background for the gold embellished table settings. This wedding is a dream; David can't find one problem with it. But he's also not looking too closely. Chicago's Cultural Center is the sort of place that makes him want to call his mom right this instant and say that there's no way he's moving back to San Jose, even though Google image searches have reminded him just how much he loves the look of a green city hemmed in by even greener mountains.

¢

Monica dances with him near the edges of the dance floor. Because the DJ has perhaps too frantic of a style, they never figure out how to dance with the music. Instead, they bob in such a way that sometimes they're close enough to touch and sometimes they're pushed away like two unfriendly magnets.

When they're close, Monica asks, "How are you liking it so far?"

He tells her it's great and that the building reminds him of his grandfather and how they used to wander the city together.

She nods, and says, "That's great." Simultaneously, she's looking over his shoulder, waving at friends. "I'm going to get a drink. You want anything?"

He shakes his head, and she leaves without so much as even touching his upper arm goodbye, and it's because of that grandpa line. Just say nice pleasant things about the wedding and about her, he reminds himself, half-mockingly. He doesn't understand why this would be different from his hotel dates with women he doesn't know, except that Monica would not be that easy.

His phone vibrates in his pocket, and when he sees the only message he's received all day, he wishes he had left the thing at home. Plane tickets, given how quickly they get expensive for international travel, have to be bought early. His mom planned ahead, didn't consult, and went ahead and bought his ticket to San Jose. The word non-refundable is clear to him in all of the fine print. The date of the flight gives him about three months to prepare, and his only chance of avoiding the move now is bad weather, and even that will only delay him for a day or less. While he's inspecting the ticket for all the detail, another vibration lets him know there's a text from his mom, too. "Can't wait to have the family all in one place. It will be good for us. Love, Mom."

Reduced to a child yet again, David has no response or recourse to his mother's actions. He can either get on the plane or not show up and risk excommunication. He knows Laurie's advice. He knows the way she wants him to put his foot down, explain his unrealized potential, and stay, blow the hundreds of dollars already invested in this new future. He doesn't have to accept every gift he didn't ask for.

The man who had trouble jumping at the park approaches

him and without much preamble asks him how he's liking the party. David, of course, tells him it's great, and he's impressed with how great of a job Monica has done. There's a silence that David has trouble filling because the flight is more important, and he doesn't know how to answer his mom. He has few options when it comes to asking appropriate small talk questions so that he can appear interested, sincere, and lively. After a second too long he settles on, "So what do you do, Pat?"

"You know those soup cans by Andy Warhol? The weird-looking artist?"

"The really, really famous artist?" David wonders if Pat is joking.

"Yeah. I don't know how famous he is, though, to people who don't have to know who he is. They did them at Target as collector's items. I helped them advertise all of that. What do you do?"

"I sort of bartend."

"Cool. Anywhere I know?"

"Club Superior? It's mostly women."

"You hook up with them a lot?" He asks with all the finesse of a nine-year-old kid.

"No. It's more my job to make sure they're happy with the club's services for bachelorette parties."

"They have strippers there?"

"We don't allow strippers."

"So what do women do at these parties?"

"Dance. Karaoke. The women who are in this wedding played board games with sex themes."

"Like what?"

"Sex Scrabble."

"That's boring. You should've gotten with one of them after."

"I sort of did."

"Who?"

"Well Monica's my date."

"Maid of Honor Monica?"

"Yeah." David thought everyone knew. Andrew had known. Even the groom said something about Monica finding a decent guy at the 11th hour in a large circle of people that included David before they left the yacht club. And a bachelorette party before the wedding is the 11th hour.

The man he's talking to now calls Monica over and waves his square hand high above his shining face. He and David stand in silence and wait while Monica winds her way through two throngs of people who all want to greet her in some way (an affect-laden kiss on the cheek, a one-armed hug, a two-hand squeeze).

"She's pretty popular. Isn't she?" David asks to cut their insulated silence.

"She is," the man replies.

"What's up, Pat?" She says when she finally extracts herself from the last hugger. "Having a good time, David?"

Before David gets a chance to answer, Pat asks, "You're on a date with a guy who babysat this bachelorette party?"

"Yes," Monica says. Her smile falters. This is not where she was planning to have this conversation. David had felt an attraction to her as she helped him clean up that night in October, but there were the undeniable conditions of their pairing, the tip she slipped him, the businesslike emails she sent with the details. She whispers in David's ear, "Can we talk about this later? We're having a great time. Why spoil it with labels?" She turns back to Pat and says, "Hope you're having a great time." Like an expert, she steers David away from Pat and toward the dance floor where the impersonal throng shields the rest of their conversation.

"I'm not talking about calling myself your boyfriend here, but this certainly feels like a date," David says.

She put a calming hand on his arm, and said, "We don't have to talk about this right now. You're having a great time. I'm having a great time. Everyone is smiling."

"How much money did this wedding cost?"

"That's beside the point."

"No, it isn't."

"Eighty grand." She gives the information up too easily,

probably because that kind of money at her disposal is probably also a point of pride.

"So about two years of my college expenses."

"Maybe. I don't know where you went to college."

"And maybe that's the problem," David says as if it's the final word on the matter.

"Look, if Pat was rude to you...I'm sorry."

"He thought I didn't know who Andy Warhol was."

"Pat barely knows who Andy Warhol is."

"Why didn't you just come alone?" But he knows she's not going to answer with even a grain of honesty if she says anything at all. "Never mind. I'm having a great time," he says after her silence.

¢

There's a woman at the bar later, not a bridesmaid but a civilian. She doesn't order a drink and appears to be content resting her arm on the glass surface and looking up at the dome, its colors muting as the sun falls behind buildings.

"What's your name?" he asks with a clumsy tongue.

"Sarah." She doesn't extend a hand or look much in his direction. He knows that she's playing it cool in exactly the same way he would be if this were a hotel situation.

"Spurned lover of the groom?"

"Distant cousin." No laugh or other acknowledgement of the joke.

"It was worth a shot," he says, shrugging.

"I'm also here mostly as a football fan, not a wedding fan."

"I'm not a football fan."

"Then you're here looking for a mate?"

"No."

A minute passes between the pair in which they look ahead. David squirms in his seat.

"I think I was hired to attend this wedding as an escort."

"Is it good money?" she asks, more interested than before.

"Think I'm breaking the terms of the contract. Don't think I'll ever find out."

He leaves without this woman's name or number.

On his way out, he finds himself passing a circle of burly men. He assumes they're football players. So he asks the question he's wanted to ask any professional athletes: "What happens if the Bears trade you?"

"We pack up and go," says one man indistinguishable from all of the others. David wishes they had their jersey numbers embroidered onto their suits. Not that it would help him much. He was always better at the sports where you had to be taller, not wider.

"You have no say in the matter?"

"Not really, just gotta bring our A games and stay useful to the team."

"I think I'm getting traded to Costa Rica," he smiles, hoping it's not too opaque.

"You play soccer, bro?"

¢

He leaves, too, without a check from Monica, or a goodbye kiss, or the promise of another date. Deflated, he gets on the blue line, sits at the windows to feel the warm air from the heaters lifting the fine hair on his arms. Thirty minutes later, he fumbles with the keys to his apartment. He turned down the heat before he left because he wasn't planning on coming home tonight, and instead of turning it up now, he doubles up on blankets and falls asleep without any trouble in a mild alcohol haze to the sound of Barb's cuckoo clocks.

In the morning, he'll decide whether it's time to cave and move home to Naperville and then to San Jose or if he'll join Laurie in an effort to postpone the move for just a few more months while he tries to save for something big like grad school. It dawns on him as one of a few remaining options: a PhD that justifies a lifetime of books, a lifetime of school where he remembers feeling comfortable and happy and well-fed with people who all believed in his ability to carve out a future for himself in the world of serious thought. It could be so different from what falls into his lap.

CHAPTER ELEVEN

Michelle

The city is undeniably in fall mode, and Michelle finds that it's not much different from the fall mode of Northern Indiana. Wreaths of reds and yellows get pinned to doors making it difficult to get close for knocking. People dig out leather boots and scarves from the backs of closets where cats sleep. When the sun shines, though, scarves and coats smell like sweat and stick to Michelle's arms when she's shoulder to shoulder with winter anticipators on the train.

She wears slippers at work now. She sweats into those, too, because the thermostat is always set to 75, which means the heat is on even in October even though she sleeps at home with her windows open. Dana says the work thermometer has to be up so high because the giant windows are big and old, but when Michelle puts her hand up to the edges of the windows, where they meet brick, she feels nothing but the comparable balminess of the sun-warmed streets. Right now, winter seems a long way off.

In the office kitchen, she inspects the snacks on her self-imposed hourly break—Michelle's eyesight is bad enough without the added strain of unbroken hours in front of computer screen—and finds a bag of chia seeds and a box of dried seaweed. The chia seeds expand in water, which means that when she tried them a few days ago, they glued themselves to the depressions in her molars and remained spongy reminders of her food experiment until she could get home to brush her teeth. She wonders how people do it, and waits in the kitchen to watch her boss, Lucas, suspend them in a small glass of water.

"Chia seeds are basically the most nutrient-rich seed in the world," he says right before he tips the glass back and lets the chia seeds slide straight down his throat without any chewing necessary.

"What's the pleasure in that?" Michelle asks. Chewing is half the fun of eating.

"You get healthy," Lucas says and maybe flexes his muscles, or maybe his shoulders have a shiver.

Michelle doesn't want to look like a naysayer. She's convinced that given the opportunity, she would learn to like them. Shopping at Whole Foods won't be as satisfying if she can't be fully enticed by the grain selection. There are many seeds she hasn't tried, and maybe even chia seeds are crunchy enough to be mixed into granola. She doesn't know, but she's excited to find out.

"You and Mark are the only two people in the office who don't like them. Have you tried adding some salt?" Lucas offers as he pours an oversized glass of ice water. Before he leaves the room, he asks, "How are your parents doing?"

"They're fine. Also, chia seeds are an acquired taste, but I'll get there."

"They called to tell me they miss you."

Michelle lowers her voice to a whisper and says, "You know I haven't told anyone we have this weird connection, right?"

"Why not?"

"Feels like nepotism."

"It's my company. I hire who I want, and when my old friend's little sister applies for a job here without my knowledge, I take that as a sign."

"I guess it's not like you groomed me for this job."

"And no offense, but anyone can learn to do what you do." He picks up his glass of water and says, "Got to get back to my office. Conference calls."

Michelle pulls out a tissue paper-thin piece of dried seaweed and breaks off a bite with her teeth. The taste is great, or the taste is green and the feeling is great, and what's left in her mouth as a translucent green film on her teeth will serve as a reminder of snack time when she runs her tongue across it. She

wishes Lucas was here to see her eat the seaweed without com-
plaint. She wishes her parents didn't have his phone number.

¢

In spite of Lucas's reminder that maybe she's somewhere she
doesn't deserve to be, Michelle exhibits a quiet confidence. She
found a job. She's making friends. She has a bedroom with a
window and some money in her bank account. It's a kind of confidence she wasn't used to. Just weeks ago, she fled a job because
of a harassment she couldn't readily explain to her parents when
it happened.

Steve, her ex-boss, had already told half the town, and she
assumed her parents knew by now even though they kept to
themselves, preferring to shop at the big anonymous Walmart
where the tourists went instead of the corner store where you
couldn't go two steps without a nod and a terse smile directed at
a neighbor or a former high school classmate. It wasn't something you really talked about in polite conversation anyway, a
young woman's breasts and their size, except there were no lim-
its to polite conversation where everyone was "essentially
family" had "known you from the time you were in diapers."

But all of that is behind her—making a scene at the diner,
storming home, packing up in a huff while her dad watched on
in abject confusion from the top of the basement stairs.

¢

She and Mark go walking after work. He shows her some of
the most ornate houses in Evanston with rolling lawns and gated
entries and the eaves painted bright colors for personality. Maybe seeing the neighborhood she works in will root her in it,
make her feel like she belongs. Mark asks her about how she
likes doing data entry, and he asks her about why she moved to
Chicago when she already had a nice deal living at home in what
he called a basement suite and she would have called a cave.

"Why don't you live at home?" Michelle shoots back at him.

"I've got Laurie."

"I kind of got the impression at the party that your relationship isn't really what it used to be." Too bold and transparent, but Mark had to know already. It was all in the way she came and asked him questions to which she already knew the answer and in the way she manufactured the bumping into each other near the fridge, and the door, and the shredder.

"It's not that it's bad. It's just different. We have real concerns now. Personally, I feel a lot less happy-go-lucky. And all of my free time is spent preparing to move on to a more suitable career."

"But Aubrey said you were going full time."

"It's what they're hoping for since I already know how the office works, but it's more complicated than that."

When Michelle doesn't say anything, Mark continues, "For us, this job is a stepping stone, and Lucas doesn't understand that."

"It's not a stepping stone for me. It's much better than what I had, and I could stay here for a long time without feeling like I'm too good for it." What she doesn't add is that she also knows the boss and this will be the path of least resistance until she can figure something else out, but she's not rushing.

"Well then what do you want to be when you grow up?" He sounds like a kindergarten teacher, full of untested optimism. Maybe he'll ask her to draw it first with stubby crayons.

"I don't know. But I wouldn't turn down a full time position just because it wasn't ideal."

"Would you do it if you felt like you weren't living up to your parents' expectations?" Mark asks, proving to Michelle just how little she knows about him. The realization gives her a jolt. He is a stranger to her in the best sense of the word.

"I'm not living up to my parents expectations." She realizes happily, too, that she doesn't have to elaborate. Mark can stay the kind of stranger she wants him to be. She can clue him in to as little or as much of her life as she wants.

"But you're not in the same city as them. This kind of gives you free reign over your life."

"Except that they still have boxes of my books."

"Let's go get them."

"Seriously?"

"Yeah. At least one of us might be able to execute a clean break."

"Now?" The books matter, but not enough. She'll feel tied to home and to pressure emanating from it for as long as she lives. But Mark wants to spend time with her, and she's not one to reject a kind of formative experience that can draw them closer together.

"Sure." He pauses. "As long as we're back for Laurie's presentation."

"It'll only take about three hours round trip. I'll have you back in time."

He's the kind of stranger who will unknowingly help her sever ties with Portage, Indiana for good.

¢

They drive south on the sprawling five lane behemoth of a highway that leads to Indiana, sticking to the local lanes where the pace is not so cutthroat and the merging from one segment of highway to another to another is made a little less complicated. Michelle promised she'd drive Mark straight home after. In some ways, Mark's right. Her parents won't be able to draw her in so easily after she picks up the remaining boxes from her cave and continues the messy work of cutting through all that connective tissue. The sunset is behind them, glaring into the rearview mirror once they turn toward Indiana and pass over the steel arch that welcomes them to the state. Crossing the border makes her feel more sluggish, less interested in the scenery that she never expects to change. But when she looks over at Mark, it seems as if he's hardly even noticed the difference. In terms of what it looks like, both the Illinois and Indiana side of the highway block views of teetering clapboard houses with elaborate wood porches on the brink of collapse.

He asks, "Can we turn the heat up?" His arm no longer warmed by the sun. And before Michelle answers, he reaches over and turns the plastic knob up to two, but the increase in fan volume is masked by the rubber, concrete, and engine sounds of the road.

Twenty miles past the Illinois-Indiana border, Michelle pulls her car into the exit lane with its familiar debris of hubcaps and the shreds of tires tangled in the low brush. She winds her way through a confusing faux grid of streets full of dead ends that stop short at overgrown rivers and fenced-in factories.

"This is my house," she says, pointing and pulling up across the street from a ranch style house built low to the ground on a small lot as small as all the others. She wants him to think it's sad, to realize what sad is, that sad is not working a data entry job.

"Your parents look like they garden." He is referring to the barrels full of dirt on the perimeter of the property. In the spring, they're planted with blooming perennials in colors Michelle forget exist during the long cold winter. Their appearance every year without fail was welcoming to her until it became oppressive, until she realized everyone got their flowers from the same garden center by the highway.

"They try." She shrugs. "Look, though, at how all the houses look the same. They're full of the same people."

"And Chicago isn't?"

"You have a girlfriend who sells breast milk."

"Sold breast milk."

"Same difference."

"Let's go get your stuff and get out of here if you can't stand it so much." He doesn't wait for an answer and opens the door to let the chilly air in.

Michelle follows, and they ring the doorbell because she took her key off of its ring and stuffed it into a shoebox full of pieces of paper she calls memories. It takes one of her parents a bit to reach the door, and she can tell they're hesitant. They've probably already seen two indistinct blobs in the decorative glass panels surrounding the door.

"Michelle. Did Lucas tell you we called?" her father asks when he opens the door.

"Yes, but I'm just here to get some more of my stuff." Michelle looks at Mark. "This is Mark. He's a coworker, and he's here to help me carry the boxes. I don't want to bother you."

"We know why you left."

"Don't."

"That kind of surgery is not the best use of your hard-earned money when we're feeding and housing you, too."

Her mother sticks her head out of the living room. Michelle knew she'd be in there reading and refusing to acknowledge the door.

"Did you tell her that we don't want her to get a boob job, Lawrence?"

"Don't call it that. It's a legitimate procedure, Mom."

Mark doesn't move. He doesn't say he'll wait in the car like he's supposed to. And in an instant, he becomes less stranger and more confidant, and a confidant she didn't need or want.

"Either way, honey. It's for people who have money and a reason to enhance themselves," her father says, clearly uncomfortable. He already assumes that Mark is her boyfriend. Why else would Michelle have brought him home? Now, she's not so sure why he's here. His arms are noodles. She'll be doing most of the heavy lifting.

"Dad. I'm not doing it. I can't anymore."

"Come home," her mom says forceful. "I can get you a job at the plant in the office. No one knows up there about what happened."

"No. I want to be in Chicago."

"You could have done it smarter."

Michelle pushes past her dad into the kitchen where the stairs to the basement are. Mark follows after exchanging some quiet niceties with her parents. She hopes he's not apologizing for her.

She feels the switches for the basement before she sees them in the darkness. They are where they've always been.

"Careful, the stairs down here are crooked," she says to Mark when she feels his presence at the top of the staircase. Together, they pick up two boxes of books already taped up.

"Big room," Mark says looking around even though Michelle is trying not to.

"Cold in the winter," Michelle replies though she is already back at the stairs, climbing up to meet her parents in the kitchen.

"We don't think this is a good idea," her father says before she's through the narrow doorway.

"It is."

"What about when Lucas finds out?"

"He won't."

They all turn to Mark coming up the stairs with heavy steps. He looks winded already and she regrets his coming.

She regrets her own coming until it's time to say goodbye. Mark waits for her in the car while she returns to her parents. They hug. Concern lines their foreheads, and it certainly lines hers, too, but if she's there and she's working, the next few steps can't be that difficult.

"I'll call more often," she says.

"Don't make us keep calling Lucas," her mom says.

When Michelle gets back in the car, Mark jumps right into it, "This is a nice neighborhood with houses that are cared for, and I don't feel so bad for you."

"Do you wish you had it?"

"Why do you think I had something different?"

"Do you want to know why I left my last job so quickly?"

"The pay was horrible and you needed the money for your boobs?"

"Yes, but also, I slashed my boss's tires for telling everyone that I was saving up for breast implants."

Mark looks down away from her face. The pair face each

other with torsos twisted in the middle with arms out to stabilize the contortion. She's sure he can't help looking down, but at least he doesn't tell her they're fine the way they are, or that she shouldn't have told her boss in the first place. Because she isn't stupid, Michelle knows all of this already.

"Ready to go back?" she asks.

"Before Laurie starts to worry about us."

"Us?" Michelle puts the car in reverse in order to back out of the dead end street.

"It's her business meeting tonight."

"Do you think it's worth it?"

Mark takes a long time to answer. They're almost to the highway when he says, "Laurie has grand ideas that never turn out the way she plans, but sometimes it's because no one expects it to work out, including me."

"You're doing the best you can," Michelle says. Her arm slides off of the steering wheel to rest on his knee. He shifts toward her a bit. They are strangers but they will share each other's secrets.

CHAPTER TWELVE

Laurie

"Come into my office," Laurie says, ushering David and Ola in through the door to her apartment.

"You've lived here for six months, and I've never seen this place during the day," David says, looking around in what Laurie hopes is appreciation. They have to believe her that she's done what she can on their shoestring budget to cover up or distract from the cracks in the walls, the sloping floors the landlord swears aren't dangerous.

Laurie tries to arrange them on the couch, but David goes for his usual spot on the floor with his feet tucked under the coffee table. Ola sits on the edge of the loveseat slightly off-kilter because she didn't bother to move the cushions. She must be nervous, Laurie thinks.

"You know more or less what the business proposition I have for you is?" She rubs her hands together for warmth. Mark turned the heat down in the morning before Laurie was even up, and she didn't want to touch it so that he would know she was serious about curtailing their expenses. But she wishes she could build a fire in the nook of their bay window.

"Not really," David says. He's looking at his nails, clearly distracted. She had tried and failed to get him in on the ground floor of the breast milk business. In retrospect, his reluctance was warranted, and she hoped that his disinterest today wasn't a sign of what would happen to this venture.

"Tell me about the wedding," she says to him.

"It was fine. Nice date, and the cultural center is beautiful," David says still not looking up.

"If you don't want to talk about it, we can just talk about the plan. It's fine, but don't blame me for how bad it was."

"Shouldn't we wait for Michelle?" Ola asks. She is disinterested in witnessing this squabble. She hasn't even introduced herself to David.

"Sure she's coming?" Laurie asks.

"She didn't come back from work, so I have no idea."

"Tell me more about the wedding," Laurie commands, realizing she hasn't really spoken with David since the party. She wants to distract herself. Mark hasn't come home from work yet, either.

"It was okay. I met some professional football players, but no one here knows their names so it's probably not that interesting."

"Did she explain what the date meant?"

"No, and she was more difficult to read than the women I'm used to, which is a not a great thing."

"What do you mean 'the women I'm used to'?"

"I mean like you," David hurries to say.

"No, you don't." Laurie knew there was something he was hiding about that job, something nefarious she wouldn't approve of.

The three sit in silence, and even Laurie and David have trouble with conversation because of this new element: a scowling Ola with arms crossed loose across her chest, her purse in her lap as if she's planning on making a run for it if this gets as weird as Laurie made it sound. In the meantime, Laurie organizes the apps on the home screen of her phone in the name of efficiency. Apps are easier to access if they are ordered by importance and frequency of use, which means that the phone icon itself gets relegated to fourth place after Facebook, Messages, and E-mail, not that there's anything wrong with this. Laurie enjoys new methods of communication and is ready to abandon at a moment's notice what isn't working.

All three perk up at the sound of someone clunking up the hollow, pine stairs. Or maybe it's two people. Or maybe it's an echo. And it doesn't take long before Michelle and Mark come through the front door. They look guilty to Laurie, and she considers a confrontation. Michelle is half an hour late, and Mark didn't text or call to say he was staying late at work. She raises her eyebrows at David but says nothing except for the obligatory "hey" that everyone shares in an overlapping chorus. It doesn't matter who started it.

"Now that we're all here let me introduce the two of you to David, my best friend," Laurie says. "This is Ola and this is Michelle."

And another chorus of "nice to meet you" follows from which Laurie can extract herself to give Mark the meanest look she can muster. Thankfully, she's wearing a wristwatch and can point at it in more than mock annoyance. But she turns back to her audience, which is complete with Michelle and the guilty expression on her face.

"What I want you guys to do is cuddle. And then you get paid. And then you leave. You never see the person again. You give me a cut, and then I set up the next one," she says when Mark is in the kitchen.

"I don't like it," Ola says.

"Why?"

"Why do you get a cut?"

They're all skeptical. They don't want to help Laurie, and they don't understand how exactly they could benefit from her business acumen.

"I'll do all the leg work. Advertising. Scheduling. Call me your 'Cuddling Coordinator.'" Laurie smiles.

"But any one of us could do that," Ola shoots back.

"It's my idea. I get to lay out the terms."

"Will you cuddle, too?" David asks.

"Of course, but I don't see how this is a big deal for you, David. From what I understand, I just described your job." She's proud of herself for that jab.

"You're asking us to do this at night," Michelle says, thinking immediately and rather selfishly of the dangers of the predator.

"But you'll be out of there by midnight, and we'll have a check-in system," Laurie replies, hoping to placate for now. She needs start-up cuddlers and then when she has some name recognition maybe she can hire real professionals who know how to treat a stranger.

"How does that work?"

"You'll text me."

"But you can't text in bed and be an attentive cuddler," David says as if he's had any experience in that department.

"No, but you can excuse yourself and text me from the bathroom."

"Naked?"

"Of course not."

"Is there a vetting process?" Michelle persists.

"What do you mean?"

"How do we know we're not hugging someone who has sexually assaulted in the past."

"I think that's probably an occupational hazard for the first few months of this business before we have a steady client base." Laurie looks around. "Is that not a risk you're willing to take for thirty five dollars an hour?" She's serious. "Look, Ola. You for instance don't actually like cleaning people's bathrooms, but you do it because you like the money. From what I understand, the money is good?"

Ola nods.

"Well, then this is the same thing. You might not like it, but you will profit."

She takes their silence as an invitation to move forward, and she pulls out her laptop, letting them weigh their safety against potential earnings silently. She assumes each one of them has a different formula for this calculation.

"Let me tell you a little story," she says to her not quite rapt audience. "When I was young, my mother encouraged me to supplement my allowance. I got five dollars a week from her when I was ten, which basically covered my trips to the 7-11 for Slurpees. When I ran out of money, I raided the family change jar, but I felt bad about when I had to switch from paying in quarters to dimes and eventually to nickels. So I decided—and I know it seems early—to make something of myself.

"I opened a lemonade stand. It was small with a cardboard box for a table. We lived on a pretty busy street, and at fifty cents a cup, I was making enough money to cover weeks' worth of Slurpees. It was a great feeling to be rewarded for the hard work I was putting in. There was cause and effect. Supply and demand.

"My mom, though, took my success as an indication that I didn't need my set allowance anymore because I could do so much better on my own. And during the summer it was fine. I would even bring home treats from the store for my mom. Mostly candy, but I felt good about it. The winter is when it got tough. No one wanted lemonade, and just like that I had to hunker down and wait for warm weather to return."

"I've heard this story before," Mark yells from the kitchen.

"It's not for your benefit." She will not let him bully her in their own apartment.

"I think I understand," Ola cuts off their spat. "You call yourself an entrepreneur, and you've been doing it for years. We're supposed to trust you."

"I'm asking you to make opportunity during the winter. The world is like my mom who never reinstated my allowance officially and I had to ask her every time I needed money."

Mark laughs from the kitchen.

¢

They put together an ad for Craigslist after a debate over which category an ad like this might be placed under. They settle on "Services Offered"(heading) "Therapeutic Services" (subheading), and post the following:

Warm Bodies Seek the Lonely and the Tired for No Strings Attached Cuddle

We live in a lonely world colored by the glow of a billion com-

puter screens, and sometimes the weight of a Snuggie just doesn't cut it.

Winter is coming. Why don't you treat yourself to a cuddle with a living, fleshy human being? All you have to do is write to us, choose your cuddler's gender, select a time, and be lulled to sleep in the arms of a young Chicagoan.

Rates are negotiable but start at 60 dollars an hour. Similar to a massage but more emotionally therapeutic and relaxing.

Email us!
PS- This is not an escort service nor does it involve sex.

The response they receive overwhelms them in the first two hours. Sure, there are lewd photos and spambot emails, but there are also ten real replies. Most messages are terse, cautious, feeling around for a way to ask questions about the legitimacy of the venture. Laurie answers each one with her three accomplices crouched around the coffee table that doubles as a desk.

While they waited, they drank and played Monopoly. Michelle won because of the alliance she forged with David. It only made Laurie angrier with her, and throughout the game, she popped into the bathroom to stare at herself in the mirror for too long as she pretended to wash her hands.

Mark watches them read the emails from the doorway to their room. He shakes his head at Laurie when she volunteers to go first. No one else objects. If they had, she may have considered moving herself down the list. She knows it's risky, but she has to inspire confidence as a de facto CEO, the shining face of the newest craze in intimacy.

From the replies, she chooses a man named Jer for herself. He seems straightforward and not too concerned with the finer points and legalities like the man she assigns to Ola. He'll probably be a bore.

After everyone leaves, Mark says, "I will not accept cuddling money from you. Please get a real job, Laurie."

"This can turn into a real job."

"Just like the breast milk was?"

"Yes. I made money. I paid for half the bills." Laurie is tired of living with unspoken accusations of her worthlessness. She sees how easy it is for Mark, how he comes home and relaxes, reads his websites, writes a little blog post about whatever interests him, and then goes to bed. She can't follow him into that office to experience the drudgery that makes his leisure possible. "I can't do what you do," she says, shrugging, knowing that she cares more about the adventure, but she cares about the adventure only when it pays off, when someone is able to marvel at her success.

"But you could do what I do with so little stress."

"But not without feeling guilty for not living up to a kind of potential I saw in myself."

Later, she asks, "Why did I pay so much for college if it feels like it taught me nothing?"

"You met me there."

"Don't side-step the question," she says surprised at her own callousness to Mark's attempt at a sweet joke.

"I don't know, Laurie. You can't return the degree."

"Class action lawsuit."

"No." He turns to leave the room. When she gets in the bed, there won't be anymore conversation, unless she wants to chat with his fake deep breathing.

"What were you doing with Michelle?"

"Nothing. We stayed late at work."

"Why? You never do that," she says. Keeping her suspicions in check is important because she'd much rather catch him in the lie organically without having to pull it out of him.

"I don't know. Lots of paperwork. Lucas wants me to go full time."

How does she muster the strength to squeeze an "I'm proud

of you" through her teeth? She mumbles it, which sounds worse than not saying it at all.

¢

Jer reschedules no longer satisfied with an evening but a mid-afternoon. He's probably more nervous than Laurie herself. She replies long after everyone has left. And before bed, she thinks of all the policies and terms she'll have to compose for the eventual website. She could have real fine print this time. Maybe it's time to look into an LLC for "Chicago Cuddlers" or "Chi City Intimates."

CHAPTER THIRTEEN

Ola

Ola is the first to cuddle, even though it was supposed to be Laurie, but Laurie texted and told her that Jer rescheduled, which leaves Ola more angry than nervous. The person who had the idea should go first. It's an old playground rule but one Ola thinks still applies to her everyday interactions. For all she knows, Laurie is lying and rescheduled the appointment herself. She rings the doorbell to an apartment that looks like it's housed in what used to be a mansion. The porch is fantastically wide, and the stone arches hold the weight of three stories of heavy masonry. She double-checks the text from Laurie for the apartment number while listening to the neighbor's wind chimes. The text itself was very cryptic: "Daniel. 1059 W Grace, Apt 4W. Prepaid on PayPal. 1 hour. 8pm." Didn't even have the decency to call with the information.

The door buzzes and she pushes hard, knowing the wood and glass will be heavy, and they are. Stairs creak in an ominous chorus under Ola's feet, and there are no lights coming from under any of the apartment doors she passes on her way up. When she knocks on the dark wood cracking and cracked in places, she hears a calm voice immediately say, "Come in."

She opens the door to find a man standing in a claustrophobic living room with only the light from the orange street lamp outside illuminating what is inside. The light hairs on his head stand up in concentrated wisps. He's already slight and the downy hair makes him look slight and young, younger than Ola even. She is relieved that he looks nothing like Alex who has a peculiar blend of chestnut brown and black hair, like he was born with highlights.

"This isn't my bed. I don't know if I want you in my bed," the man says by way of introduction as he points to a fold out couch with a gray sheet draped across it.

"That's fine."

The man sits and pats the mattress next to him in a move that is part attempt at seduction and part nervous tic. Reluctantly, Ola joins him. They're not touching yet, and it feels like there's a force field keeping them from each other, which Ola hopes will hold for the remainder of the hour. This apartment does not smell like Ola's. This man's sheets are stale, and that should be the least of her concerns. Why won't he turn the light on? She imagines his face covered in boils that secrete a green pus, but she doesn't turn her head to check. That would be impolite, or worse, it might imply that she's ready for this. There's a clock somewhere deep in the apartment that ticks just like hers. It's a steady rhythm, which reminds her that she still belongs to a world where she can walk out on this if she needs to. She's lucky enough to not need this money to feed herself. She recognizes that maybe Laurie is not so lucky.

"Are we getting under the sheet or are we laying on top of it?" she asks, finding it better to talk than to stare at a blank wall.

"I don't know. I get kind of sweaty in bed and think it might be best for both of us if we're not under them."

Ola keeps her jacket on. "Do you mind?" She asks before stiffly laying down next to him.

"I don't know how to negotiate this. Do you know how?"

For a few minutes, they are an awkward mess of limbs that don't necessarily want to touch. Every accidental grazing has to be apologized for, and this man's skin is already damp. She forgot his name immediately after reading the texted assignment from Laurie, and now, on this lumpy mattress, it's too late to ask.

"I'll start my egg timer now," he says.

Ola thinks that might be a little too precise, but she says, "okay" so that he knows she's not asleep.

She lets her mind wander while she feels this stranger's chest rise and fall in a forced cycle to calm him or both of them.

Michelle and David are cuddling tomorrow, too. What she imagines for them is similar but maybe brighter. She wonders if any of them will fall asleep, or if this is supposed to be half an hour of spooning and then another half an hour of being spooned, or if Ola should have told this guy that his time was ticking away from the moment she walked through the door.

She feels that she has only herself to blame. Alex asked her to move, and she refused even though she knew it was stubbornness and fear holding her back in the city. Her parents asked her to get a job and she relented only when she felt someone else was infringing on her independence at work, namely, her employer. She wanted gigs to cobble together cash, and this cuddling is even more of a gig than she had bargained for when she first started imagining a life of cleaning houses, freelance editing, acting, holding signs on street corners. She is in bed with a man who thinks she's too morally unclean to invite into his bed when he's the one surfing Craigslist for a cuddle buddy. Indignation bubbles up inside of her and comes out of her skin in goosebumps on her calves. This does not feel like any cuddle she ever experienced. The closest is maybe the one time she and Alex slept in her dorm room when her roommate was around. No one could get to sleep, and she spent the whole night listening to the rustling of sheets. It's not that she was embarrassed. The roommate was an unknown element. Neither she nor Alex planned for her to be there, and they had scrambled to put clothes on when she walked in, made small talk until it was clear that Claire wanted to turn off the lights.

She squirms. She tries to pull all the warmth into the center of her body as if it were a ball she could protect with flesh. Warmth or soul or whatever you might want to call it. She doesn't want this nameless man having any access to it. Over in the corner is a pile of clothes in all grays.

When the egg timer goes off, she sighs in relief.

"Yeah. I can't say I liked that as much as I thought I would," he says, sitting up like a bolt.

"Then I guess we can agree on that.

¢

Her parents surprise her at the apartment, driving the car she wants from them. They offer her the Volvo to congratulate her on the new job. But they make her come over to their house after work tomorrow to stay the night and sort out how the transfer of the title will work. It's all stuff they could handle over the phone, but this is a treat, and she doesn't want to upset them. They bring a cheesecake, and she has to dig down in the bottom cabinet for a serving tray, which her mom is convinced she threw away or gave to Alex when he left. But it's there underneath a greasy cookie sheet and a mismatched set of small pots and pans.

Her parents have bright faces. Ola knows they are happy that they can finally give her a gift of this size. They tell her so, and they apologize again for leaving her with some student loan debt, and she tells them it's fine. Now, her two jobs will keep her living in luxury. Maybe she'll get an auxiliary cord installed in the car so that she can listen to music off her phone or mp3 player.

"But promise us you'll quit the cleaning."

"I can't quit until I know they're keeping me at the office."

"Bill would never fire you. He's our friend."

"He might."

"Just don't give him a reason to," her mother says, assuming her guilt before she's had a chance to do anything wrong.

But Ola promises. She wants the freedom of the car. She wants the responsibility of it, too.

Later, when she's in bed, rubbing her feet together for warmth, refusing to turn the heat on just yet, wondering when she'll hear Michelle struggling to find her keys in the cavernous purse she slings over one shoulder, Ola considers her plan:

- Drive to parents' house.
- Show them proof of insurance.
- Stay the night, quietly planning trip to Seattle on old

desktop computer weighing down spindly childhood desk [clear the history after just in case].

- Drive home whenever, no need for bus tracker.
- Call Bill and reschedule start date at the office.
- Imply family illness in order to cancel houses for next week.

Ola gets in a list mood when she starts thinking in bullet points so she gets out a pen and paper to start planning her trip before sleep. And when the preliminary planning is done (a budget outlined in pencil, a tentative schedule, a mock script of what their first meeting might sound like), Ola is too awake to just waste time in bed.

Taking advantage of Michelle's absence, Ola decides to take a hot bath with more bubbles than she's had since her dad would pour in so much soap that she looked like she was floating in a pool of meringue.

CHAPTER FOURTEEN

Michelle

She doesn't want to cuddle and have to re-arrange her body around another body in a strange part of the city she's never seen. She doesn't want to be drunk when she does it, but she also doesn't want to be sober. Laurie told her not to drink because she wouldn't be able to protect her that way. And Michelle thinks that was a little melodramatic until she is about to knock on the door of the person who needs her hugs and remembers that there are only three other people (and maybe Mark) on this planet who know where she is, what kind of danger she's putting herself in, and she can't do it.

But that's Indiana talking, she reasons. This is more or less what she came here to do, find a way to live without other people telling her what to do. She wants to be anonymous again.

She is here to try new things. She is here to get in on the ground floor of a dynamic new business that caters to the young professional who doesn't need the hassle of a relationship but wants the warmth of someone in their bed who isn't demanding sex, who is refusing sex, in fact, in all of its messiness and distraction. What it is is urban.

She stands on the new carpet of this high rise downtown where the walls in the hallways are a pleasant slate gray and there's a bunch of lavender on the accent table by the elevator. So calming. So spa-like.

The woman who opens the door is not naked, but she's not dressed either, holding out her hand to Michelle as if she wants Michelle to kiss it. "Luella's the name." A southern accent, forced and hackneyed, probably fake.

"I'm Darcy," Michelle says. "Your Cuddling Specialist." Laurie insisted that they pick fake names, and she thought it would be silly, until she met this Luella who stands with a hand on her hip, like a caricature of a demanding girlfriend with her whole body pitched forward. There was no way to tell if this was a standard beginning to one of these. Earlier in the day, Ola didn't want to talk about what had happened with her cuddling appointment. She was in the bathtub when Michelle came home, and when her water got cold, Michelle heard her let a little bit out to make room for some more of the scalding stuff. After an hour of silence, Michelle asked if everything was all right, and received only the tersest reply in return.

"Luella" wants to have a drink first. Her bar cart contains every kind of glassware imaginable. Michelle remembers that not even the restaurant she worked for had this large of a collection of anything, and no one expects a good cocktail or smooth glass of wine at a diner anyway. She maybe wouldn't have left if that were the case. Even though Michelle knows she shouldn't accept, the bottles gleam the same way Luella's eyes do. So she says yes and tries to forget Laurie's rule book. She will do this her way.

After one drink she says, "My real name is Michelle."

"My real name is Luella, but it wasn't my birth name. Do you think it's time to start?" Without waiting for an answer, Luella disappears around the corner.

Michelle takes her phone out of her purse and puts it in the kangaroo pocket of her pullover hoodie before following Luella. Her bedroom is a soulless cube, just a place to put a bed and a dresser. Her window is small and cracked open just to let a little bit of cool air in, which is its only function given that it provides nothing but a view of the red brick of the building next door, similar in size, utility, and occupant.

"Get in here," Luella says. "I plan on taking full advantage of this hour."

"Well, if that's the case, I should run to the bathroom. Where is it?"

Luella points to a door directly behind Michelle. Old rose wallpaper curls in on itself near the ceiling line, evidence of a moisture problem, and she knows that all of Luella's throw pillows and stacks of towels, and overflowing bar cart are there to mask the disrepair of the place itself. The apartment Michelle now occupies hasn't revealed its maintenance secrets yet; she'll find the leaks in no time.

Luella has not touched her without permission. Hasn't broken the rules sent to her by email before this meeting. She just has lecherous eyes that make Michelle feel like she romanticized her motives before meeting her.

From the bathroom she texts Laurie: "This is getting weird. How do I get out early?"

Laurie doesn't respond.

She texts again but knows that Luella will start to wonder if she stays in this cramped bathroom any longer. She flushes the toilet for effect, runs the faucet, wets her hands, and towels them off. In the mirror she sees that she's overdressed. The leggings and long-sleeved shirt were meant to minimize skin-on-skin contact, but now she feels like she's wrapped herself in a shroud, particularly compared to the cotton romper with spaghetti straps on Luella. It's definitely a sleeping get up for a different season and a different level of intimacy. But on the other hand, the worst thing to do for business would be to make Luella feel unwanted, unhuggable. As a compromise, Michelle hikes up her sleeves to reveal her freckly arms. Perhaps that twelve inches of skin will make a difference and mollify Luella. Or maybe Luella will sense the apprehension in Michelle's eyes, the slight wrinkle at the top of her eyebrow and relent, suggest they try again another time.

Before Michelle opens the door, she texts Mark too: Luella's address, and below it, she writes, "just in case."

Back in the bedroom, Luella strips down to her underwear, instructs Michelle to do the same.

"I don't know if that's really something I can do according to the rules you were emailed."

"It's a one-time experience. I'm not asking you to keep coming back," Luella says as she gets under the covers. "I've already paid you."

"I know."

"It's less than an hour at this point."

Michelle starts by pulling her sleeves back down so that her shirt is easier to take off. Luella watches and waits.

When they're both in bed, Luella's breathing relaxes, her eyes flutter shut, and within minutes she's asleep. Michelle doesn't move, though, for fear of waking her and hopes she can maintain her pose (fetal position, little spoon) for the next forty minutes.

Without a clock to reference or anything to read, Michelle is bored enough to start imagining what her day would've looked like had she never left Portage, Indiana: a small breakfast at the kitchen table lit by one overhead light, leaving for the morning shift at the diner before her parents woke, a long string of customers more demanding than Luella in some ways, followed by a shift meal, followed by hours in front of the television. She doesn't want to return, but she knows this, too, doesn't look like what she imagined when she considered life in the city.

The phone she positioned near her pillow remains silent. Laurie has decided to not keep her promise and protect her. Mark is no better, but he didn't promise her a thing. She would never have asked.

When she's done, she texts Laurie one more time: "I'm alive."

On her way to the train, she runs into Mark walking in her direction alone. Trees damp from the day's drizzle shake leftover droplets into their hair when they stop.

Without allowing for niceties, she asks, "What are you doing here?"

"You texted me, and I thought it was an SOS. I came as soon as I could." His hair is sticking to his forehead.

"I'm done already." Michelle can't help but feel a little petulant. If this had been a serious emergency, Mark would have been too late. He could've taken a cab.

"Sorry I couldn't come sooner," he repeats.

"It's okay."

"I was on a date with Laurie."

"That's fine. She's your girlfriend." Michelle, of course, doesn't believe it's fine. She believes instead that Laurie deliberately made herself busy.

Together, they start walking in the direction of the train.

"It's not fine," Mark says. "I didn't want to be with her."

Michelle knows that he's implying that he'd rather be with her. Flattery is not what she's looking for.

"Thank you for coming to see if I was okay."

"I can take the train back home with you. Make sure you get there without a problem."

Discomfort hangs between them as heavy as the wet air.

"Does Laurie know you're here?"

He looks down at his gray running shorts and dark blue wind breaker. "No. Why do you think I'm dressed like this?"

"I should take the bus," Michelle says, turning away from him to walk back to the corner they just passed.

"It'll take you three times as long to get home."

"I know."

He doesn't understand that she would rather be alone than with someone who expects something from her—whether it's a hug, or a cuddle, or just a secret kept quiet.

"I'm breaking up with her," he says. He follows her to the bus stop, which is just a pole anchored in cracked concrete, topped with a peeling blue and white sign.

"That's great." She steps into the empty street for a better view.

"I'm serious." And after a pause, "Told her I was going running so that I could come to see you." he says.

She says nothing in return. She puts her hands in her pockets, and she winds up looking a little hunched over and closed off.

"Let me at least text the bus for you to see if it's worth waiting in the dampness."

"Okay."

She watches as he fiddles with the giant screen he keeps in his pocket, opening a field for a new text message, struggling to transcribe the long strings of numbers from the bus stop above his head to his phone. She doesn't help him read. There isn't a rush to get back to her closet of a room.

The text comes and it claims there's a bus approaching even though they can neither hear nor see it.

"I guess I'll leave you be then."

"Hope you understand that I'd just rather be alone."

"I'm risking my relationship here with you." His tone can't be described as threatening.

Plaintive is a better word like he thought this was the best he could do, and then having exhausted his option, all that's left is some light pouting.

 The bus saves her. Its doors sigh open, and she steps onto the wide ramp before she thanks him again with only a half turn back to face him.

Mark is wrong, too, about how long it should take her to get home. This bus driver knows she's his only fare for the time be-ing, and he somehow senses her urgency, blowing through yellow lights, barely registering the empty bus stops peppered along the route. For such a big city, Chicago has a tendency to look less congested than it really is, especially in the late fall when everyone is dreading winter and they're not yet sick of watching television every night.

Her almost apartment is empty, and Ola has left a note in her scratchy angular handwriting about going to her parents' house for the night and then maybe leaving for Seattle in the morning, but that she'll probably have to come home to pack still. Michelle is convinced she has misread it, but maybe not. Maybe this cuddling drives most of us to do crazy things to seek out re-al intimacy again, which might be the only cure for being exposed to the fake stuff. She's worried about what she might try if she lets herself.

CHAPTER FIFTEEN

David

David, upon walking through the door to her building and into a metallic but warm lobby, feels that he has found his match in this cuddler. She lives in a Gold Coast high rise. He gives her name to the doorman who has eyes on the physical door and a number of screens showing him views of other doors. On the screen, they all look alike and unmolested, but he still has to make physical rounds once an hour. A lonely activity, David imagines.

He says "thank you" to the man who is looking everywhere but at him.

In the elevator, he wonders if he hasn't stepped into a dream. The walls are covered in a futuristic, undulating plastic with a basket-weave texture in a blood red. It feels smooth to the touch, and cold. Someone steps into the elevator after David and interrupts his fondling of the wall. He wears the same distressed jeans and the same flannel with sleeves rolled up but in a different pattern, more muted colors. He doesn't have David's watch, though. And David's watch is awesome with its thick leather band and beige face snapped in and little wooden arrows pointing at no numbers, just silver notches. They do not speak. David doesn't trust himself to not say why he's here if pressed.

He convinces himself that the hallway is nothing special. Once you've seen one textured blood wall, you've seen them all. And when he knocks on apartment 1103, he manages to arrange his face so that he looks bored: a downward cast to the eyes and mouth, fingers picking absently at a hairline.

"Hi," she says before she shows herself in the frame of the door. "Thanks for doing this," she continues in the contemporary version of a mid-atlantic accent, so close to what David imagines to be British, like she just hopped across the pond for a decent haircut, which she has in the form of cascading, full waves and a manicure the color of thin ice in the sun. She's old enough to know it's hard work to look this effortlessly young.

Her apartment is beautiful, too. All he needs to see is a sliver of it over her shoulder, but it's so soft. It's all the colors of the wedding that he doesn't want to think about anymore. He feels that this is permanent, though. Not a monument to beauty and wealth erected for just the afternoon, this is as permanent as the Tiffany dome. He'll want to check and see if the light gray couch is bolted to the floor, like he imagines they do in mansions that double as museums.

"Do come in," she says politely.

When he's settled on the couch, which still shifts under his weight, she breaks another silence by saying, "forgive the mess."

"Is Zibbette your real name?" he asks. Couldn't have picked a worse first line. Of course it's not her real name. Zibbettes don't own Gold Coast apartments, and women who own Gold Coast apartments don't use their real names when surfing Craigslist for a partner.

"Unfortunately, it is," she laughs.

"Is it short for anything?"

"No." She laughs again. "People always ask me that, and I usually say 'It's short for my parents have a really hazy conception of the real world.'"

Now, David laughs. Not because it's a great joke, but because she's self-aware. She knows Zibbette is silly. He has permission to think it, too.

"Is David your real name?"

"Yeah. It is, but it's pronounced the un-American way. Like da-veed. I'm not from here." He doesn't pull this card too often, doesn't need to, but here, he needs to match Zibbette, and he gets the feeling she probably has a taste for the exotic.

"It's beautiful," she replies.

"But to be honest with you, it reminds me of something I don't really want to think about."

"What is it?" she asks, almost gasping, horrified that something unpleasant might be able to touch her all the way up here where clouds sometimes form to skitter playfully between buildings.

"I might have to leave Chicago."

"Here, tell me about it in bed. It's better anyway if we have something to talk about," said like she's the expert.

Zibbette pours him a drink (an unfussy bourbon on the rocks) without asking. She pours herself the same thing, lifts the two glasses off the counter, and leads David into her bedroom, setting a glass on each of the boxy, brass nightstands.

"You can have the side by the door so that when you're spooning me, you'll still have a view of the skyline."

In fact, David had been too busy watching her slim, steady arms to notice that they had walked into a room with a wall of windows and an almost unobstructed view of the curve of the lake and the twinkling lights of the park below.

"You fall asleep to this every night?" he asks, feeling dumb before the words leave his mouth.

"Actually, I have a spot of insomnia, so I fall asleep just when the sun is rising over the water."

"Maybe it's not insomnia. Maybe you just like the view."

"That kind of talk makes me want to move." She slides into bed with all of her clothes still on, the fleecy socks, the leggings, the oversized t-shirt draped just right over her small, bony shoulders.

David follows, but first, he removes the heavy plaid flannel because of how he knows it will bunch behind his back once he gets under the covers. In just a t-shirt, he can feel the silkiness of her satin sheets and then the warmth of Zibbette's body as she presses against him. He wonders as he strains to hear the hum of Lake Shore Drive below if the warmth is her own or a kind of ambient warmth of the moment. If it's not coming from her body, then it's like the kind of warmth that comes off of some chemical reactions, a perfect melding whose first indicator is heat, like plaster getting mixed, like how he could cast this whole apartment in plaster to make a life-size replica to walk in and out of the memory. Everything he had wanted so badly to feel at the wedding, he feels now.

He sighs.

"It's nice isn't it? To be here in bed and think about nothing in particular," Zibbette purrs.

"I'm still thinking."

"About that thing you mentioned?"

"Yeah."

"Don't worry. You'll figure it out."

"This one's not really up to me."

"What do you mean?"

"If my mom decides to move and I have no good reason to stay, I'll have to go with her."

"What have you tried so far?"

"Not much. I have a shit job—"

"Hey, you're not allowed to tell me you aren't enjoying this." She pulls away slightly and takes some warmth with her.

"No. Not this. This is really nice." With open arms, David co-axes her a little closer. "My day job that's actually a night job is chaperoning bachelorette parties."

"Sounds a little bit like fun."

"I think it could be for the right kind of guy, but my family doesn't respect it, and I guess I don't really either." Concise, but more honest than anything he's said or thought before meeting Zibbette.

"This is different?"

"I don't know yet. You're my first cuddle."

Zibbette raises an eyebrow. "I've heard that before."

And David has said a variation of it before to a few women without meaning it, without feeling the warmth of tonight.

"That doesn't make it less true right now."

They settle back into a quiet half-sleep. Or Zibbette is half-sleeping. David is concentrating on matching his breathing to hers, which is one of the most thoughtful and romantic things he can do in bed with someone. Perhaps this one will notice the attempt, snuggle closer in appreciation.

He doesn't want to play this game of wishful thinking any-more, but this wishful thinking is the best bout of wishful thinking yet. He imagines the two of them on a beach, and it's easy to replace Monica with Zibbette who would fit perfectly on a beach towel without even having to bend her legs.

"What will you do?" Zibbette asks, drawing circles on her own arm with a lazy finger.

"I have just under three months to find a job or I'll have to leave for Costa Rica with my family."

"What's in Costa Rica?"

"I guess it's a kind of home."

She sits up, folded knees up against her chest, and looks at him. "All this angst because you're moving to a tropical para-dise?"

"I'm not vacationing. I have to work there." He's sharper in his response than he expected. He feels so close to Zibbette, and he wants her to understand why he's so upset, how nobody asked for his input, how he can't be an adult unless someone else decides that what he does is worthwhile. What if hugging Zibbette every night for money, or for no money, is worth-while? He should be able to make that call himself, but he can't.

"You want to make your own way and prove to your family that you can hack it here."

"Yes."

"Well maybe you can't. Not yet." She smiles encouragingly. "It took me a long time."

"Did you go to college?"

"I did, but I didn't finish. When I left, it felt like I had gotten all I could out of an education."

"I think all I need is a real job," he concedes, abandoning the dream of more school before it had fully materialized as a plan. If Zibbette didn't need school to end up here maybe he won't need it either.

"If you were in Costa Rica, I might have more of a reason to visit."

"If I lived here, you could just hop on the blue line."

He is uncomfortable now with how far it has gone, as if Zibbette, a woman he met forty minutes ago, could care either way where he ends up in three months. The conversation sounded much better in his mind. This is a jumble, but at least he doesn't have to worry about decoding Zibbette. She says what she thinks and doesn't worry about the repercussions for anyone around her, which he realizes is both good and bad, but he likes knowing where he stands with someone who is both interested enough and rich enough to visit him in a foreign country or a country foreign to her.

"Maybe too soon," he says, feeling goosebumps on his arms and not wanting what he said to be true. Can she feel his worry through their clothes?

"Maybe yes." She shrugs one shoulder. The other one is still trapped underneath her, and she is making no moves to show David that she wants him to leave. "But this is nice."

Fifteen minutes later, the detangling is something David does reluctantly. Zibbette is relaxed by now and not holding a weight back somewhere in her torso because her body feels heavier in his arms. When she sits up on the edge of the bed, facing her view, she picks up her bourbon, now diluted, and tips the glass back to take a sizable sip. David does the same, not wanting to appear wasteful.

"Funny how we forgot about these," she says after he puts his glass back down with a clunk.

"I know. I'm usually too quick with my drinks," David replies.

"Take your time," she says, getting up, and her footsteps recede into the kitchen.

He takes another sip. Within it are cold and warm zones as if the alcohol and ice water were only now introduced to each other in his mouth. But he only has to give the glass a shake to make the whole drink homogenous in temperature. It's what he needs now that the sweat has had an opportunity to course down his calf from behind the knee.

He needs to say goodbye carefully, make sure he's leaving the door open for something more even if it is temporary. He knows now that it will be temporary because he's realizing that temporary might be all that he's ready for, too. The city says its goodbyes in the form of a beautiful view. The city knows it will be beautiful long after he leaves it. In a moment, he is at the window, not caring what it will look like to Zibbette. His hands are on the glass. Fog forms around their heat outlining his fingers. It's the closest he'll get to a handshake. And the Sears Tower way over on the right and the smiling curve of the lake and everything in between look back at him expecting nothing more.

"Are you finished with that glass?" Zibbette asks from the kitchen, her voice soft.

"I'll be right in," he replies, gathering his shirt and using the sleeve to wipe up the ring of water the glass left behind. He dims the lights in her room and pulls the door shut halfway.

"Thought you may have fallen asleep in there," she says.

"Just taking in the view."

"I would like to see you again," she says, facing away from him at the sink. "In a more relaxed way. Like a date where I don't have to pay you to hug me."

"I've heard that one before."

"Have you really?"

"Not exactly those words, of course." David smiles at her, doesn't have to worry about doing the difficult part himself.

Zibbette leads him to the door, and then she hooks both of her arms under his armpits and squeezes his ribs hard enough that he doesn't know how hard to squeeze back, but he does rest his chin on the top of her head.

"I'll see you soon," he says.

"Wait here a second." She disappears back into the apartment and returns with an envelope. "I know it feels sleazy, but I do have to pay you just this once."

"I know. It's okay." And he's not affronted. And he knows exactly what it means.

¢

The next day he knocks on Barb's door to hand her a rent envelope and some news. He waits patiently with his hands clasped in front of him as Barb undoes all of the locks from top to bottom.

"Come in, David," she says. "Would you like some tea?"

David nods, says yes, and moves to sit on the plastic-clad couch, pausing to admire the fabric underneath for the first time. Each thread of the floral design is a slightly different color, expertly matched to the others to create a soft gradient.

He can hear Barb moving in the kitchen, but the sounds are faint. No clanging pots and pans or slamming cupboard doors. Her sounds are practiced ones: boiling water, the setting of the sugar bowl on a wooden tray, turning the gas off just as the kettle starts to sing.

David gets up when he knows it's time to carry the tray in. It's the polite thing to do. He knows that much, but Barb doesn't let him. Even though her arms shake enough to make the porcelain lid on the teapot rattle.

"I'm fine, I'm fine," she says, and successfully, she sets the tray on the low coffee table. She settles down opposite David, arranges her skirt and finishes off her small movements by saying, "Help yourself."

"Thank you." He prepares his teacup backwards by filling it with a teaspoon of sugar then a few drops of lemon juice out of its little yellow orb and finally the tea when he is sure it has finished steeping.

"This is an unexpected visit," Barb says, cutting to the end of the conversation and leaving no room for the small talk he wanted to use as padding.

"I came by to drop off next month's rent early since I had it ready ahead of time." He wanted to add: thanks to some strange but rewarding almost prostitution cuddling. But he recognizes there's no need to rile up the woman who showed on her face all that he was thinking already about his job as a babysitter for drunk women. He continues to the real point when he sees that Barb is still waiting. "I also am leaving this apartment and permanently moving in with my family in three months."

"In the suburbs?" she asks, surprised.

"No. In Costa Rica, actually."

"You ever lived there?" Her way of asking if that was his country of origin. He can spot the question in all its forms.

"When I was young. I was born there."

"Are you a citizen here, though?"

"Yes. Have been for almost ten years." His answer is snippy. He doesn't appreciate the insinuation.

"So you'll still be able to visit Chicago."

He realizes that he misunderstood her tone in the same way that he misunderstood Monica's. Barb had more than a tenant. She had a life to follow with as much interest as one might follow a television show. The realization endeared her to him in a way that none of her other eccentricities could.

"It is a one-way ticket you have," she says without a question mark.

David nods.

"It will be difficult. Every change is difficult."

David sips his tea to avoid answering. The cuckoo clocks start going one by one, each has a different tune to sing on the hour, and they're set deliberately so that there's no interference. Instead of a cacophony, they perform a concert, one he's heard before when he bothered to listen closely through his (Barb's) tiled ceiling. He will miss their song.

CHAPTER SIXTEEN

Ola

Ola maps her trek to Seattle. Not too many hours. 30 hours. Optimistically, she'd do it in two days, but she budgets for three and bundles up hotel and gas cash into her open suitcase. She street views 1-90 through South Dakota until she falls asleep drooling on her flat pillow. Dreams of roads running off cliffs keep her waking every forty minutes, and she wouldn't be upset about it if the dreams themselves weren't so easy to decipher. Her mother tells her weekly of her own dream about alligators falling from the sky into shallow pools of green water surrounded by a graveyard of teeth. Ola has heard this so many times that she sometimes hears the sounds of those alligators tumbling from the sky (an angry whoosh and then a flat stone dropping into a shallow pool) before she falls asleep. Even though it's the kind of nonsense Freud lived for, she could go for a dream like that. It would be decipherable only with a long, complicated key to her subconscious and not just a quick glance at her schedule.

She told Alex about the trip, choosing to focus her email on the future instead of the failed cuddle, the implicit infidelity. It would have made more sense to surprise him for full effect and make it clear through action that she's ready now to admit a kind of defeat. She's willing to make some small sacrifices, and she's also willing to be the hero who cleans up the squalid apartment she expects to find without having to be asked. He'll call it love; she'll call it her penance.

She hasn't told her parents yet on the other hand, even though they'll eventually find out, given the 4,000 miles she is about to put on the Volvo in the course of a week. But when she goes down there next, she'll feel out the situation to see if they're happy enough about the new job to admit that she deserves a frolic or if they'll tell her to give up on Alex and look for another man in Chicago, completely misunderstanding her desire to visit, which she is still ready to argue is more about her than it is about Alex.

A road trip is the mark of success. Having the time to drive means she has the time for leisure. She isn't interested in speeding there and back, in making excuses for the journey, in counting her pennies because she finally feels like she will have enough of them. And maybe it's Alex who needs to be enticed back home.

The next morning she sets off before rush hour traffic begins, before the crush of taxis heading out to O'Hare overwhelms the four lanes, and before she backs out. On the floor underneath the passenger seat, she placed the box of Alex's leftover papers and mementos. In a way, this trip will save her some shipping costs. Never mind the 500 dollars in fuel she's ready to spend. In fact, she can hardly pretend that the box is the reason for the trip. Michelle had to remind her to take it as Ola tried to make her way down the stairs in one go with a suitcase, backpack, a loose pair of shoes, giant bottle of water, new box of tissues for the car, and a window cling to represent her alma mater on the road.

¢

It's exhausting, the drive, even in a car she thought was her dream. The backs of her thighs are asleep, the small of her back aches, her feet are too warm even when she finally slips off her shoes and is driving only in socks. She doesn't know how to work the cruise control. Or she does know how to use it in theory but is afraid that the mechanics of it just might fail her. When the heat is on, her nostrils dry up, but when it's off, cold air leaks in through the inevitable cracks quickly enough that she hears a whistling over the hum of the pavement. At rest areas, she closes her eyes and still sees the lines disappearing into the corners of her windshield where her dad told her they'd be when he first taught her to drive. It's all so familiar to her even though she has never driven cross-country and she never made it west of the Mississippi in twenty years of living in Chicago. The Minnesota countryside looks just like the one back in Illinois with fewer leaves at this time of year, but she imagines the summer green of the prairie that looks like it was taken straight out of a Windows 2000 desktop screen image. The one with the rolling hills her parents never bothered changing after she reinstalled their operating system for the tenth time.

In spurts, the big thoughts come to her. There's the big thought about the relationship: ended too soon, never really ended in the first place; the big thought about the nature of her work: doesn't count unless your hands get dirty, doesn't count unless you get tired, doesn't count if you don't get paid; the big thought about Michelle: stranger living in my apartment, on the surface more successful than I will be. This last big thought catches Ola off-guard because she's driving a mark of surface success, a beautiful car she's dreamed of for years, but even if she pulls up to all of her houses in the Volvo, even if she keeps her hair cut smooth, the highlights contemporary, she will be someone unsuccessful to her employers. And her employers, ironically she thinks, might be more unhappy. They don't have the leisure time for a car trip on a whim, they don't always have tangible goals at work, and they're never happy with their cars. Under the surface, Ola has figured something out about her own happiness. Her hands are tied up at the steering wheel so she cannot tweet or text. Instead, she tries to focus her energy on passing the eighteen wheelers that swerve off to the right when the overworked drivers doze in an energy drink haze.

¢

She sees him for the first time in six months leaning out a window smoking a hand-rolled cigarette. His hair is short, black, newly-cut. Instead of looking down at the street and at Ola, he's lost in the façade of the building across from his. She can't see into those windows, doesn't know what's so interesting inside there. She rings the buzzer for his door after double-checking the numbers above it and watches his head disappear. His voice is a distant cough through the speaker.

"It's Ola," she says. They are her first words all day except for the coffee she ordered from a disembodied voice in a drive-thru.

"Seriously? Did you even stop to nap?" It's almost difficult to hear his response through all the static.

"Yes. Please let me up. I've been driving all day."

It's a beautiful lobby with a red couch against a wall, below a painting of crashing waves. Sunlight glimmers in it as if the whole thing was real, as if it were possible in this cloudy low-ceilinged metropolis. The stairs look clean but too dark for her so she presses the button for the elevator even though she's on-ly going up to the third floor.

Alex is waiting for her when the elevator pings and opens onto a dingier hallway. He envelops her in a bear hug. Her face is level with his collarbone, less sharp than she remembered it. She softens, forgets the tension she felt in the car.

They kiss, and it's clumsy. She doesn't know who initiated, but if she had to guess, she would say Alex. Before the doors of the elevator slid open, she was sure she didn't want to touch him, but she let it happen. Even now, she can't enjoy but has to scrutinize from an imagined distance. She can't tell most of the time how far removed she is from herself.

"Come down to the car with me," she says. "I need to bring up my things."

"Yes. You are empty-handed."

She surprises herself by thinking that the nervousness and the not knowing what to say or what tone to strike are sweet. She never saw it in his polished and clear emails or terse text messages.

Together, they have no trouble carrying up her heavy bags, but she neglects to mention the most important box for him she has waiting under the seat.

"Hope these bags mean you're planning on staying a while," he says.

They sit and "fill each other in"—which sounds so proprietary when Ola considers the literal implications, but it feels almost farcical to her, this whole trip, the way in which they will invariably bump heads while leaning in to the chip bowl Alex set out on the coffee table. And then will she sleep on the couch? Will he stand over her while she's dreaming and his eventual stumble into all of the night's beer bottles will wake her, and she'll feel compelled to "cover-up" even though she plans on wearing an old scratchy t-shirt (but no bra) and does it even matter? But in this hypothetical situation, she'll have forgotten that they've seen each other naked, and as she's gathering her things and asking about a pair of leggings and her copy of The goddamn Hobbit—the one she stole from the public library by her parents' house—she'll open a closet, searching in vain and out will pop a woman or a blow up sex doll she thinks is a dead woman. Alex will have to scream "I'm not a murderer" at the top of his lungs and mind you this is the middle of the night we're imagining here in a new construction with paper-thin walls.

What actually happens is that Alex offers her his bed (he can take the couch, no problem, no really) after a pleasant two hour conversation that covers more than their emails did in all of this time. It doesn't even feel good for Ola to admit that her new job is well-paying and easy, but he's happy for her, stops the conversation for another hug.

She insists on taking the couch. The sheets Alex uses to make her bed are clean-smelling like a bouquet of dried Lavender, and she knows it's her detergent he's been using, doesn't mention the discovery, thanks him with a catch in her throat.

She insists that she needs nothing else.

Overnight, there are no surprises, just some clocks ticking, probably one at his bedside and one in the kitchen. Alex always hated the red glow of her digital, but at least it was silent. She can't tell if it's the clocks or the rolling she feels in her body, but she isn't getting much sleep. It's as if a boat had tossed her around on the waves all day, but the imaginary waves don't sound like the ocean she wants to touch tomorrow; they sound like the engine of her car. She was never once worried that the engine would die on her. There was no strange sputtering or unbearable protest when she met the eastern side of the Rockies, and the roomy gas tank held enough juice for her bladder to get full in between stops.

Before she knows it, it's morning, and Alex is offering breakfast. Ola tries to help by standing in the kitchen and trying to anticipate and provide what he'll need next for his scrambled eggs and toast, but his kitchen is arranged opposite from how they had it set up in Chicago, and they're always bumping into each other.

"Sorry," she says for what feels like the tenth time.

"It's okay. The eggs will get done either way." He looks at her briefly to smile and then falls back into working on a breakfast he perfected during their time together.

When they sit down to eat on the couch, the food is delicious. Fluffy eggs, bread toasted on the lighter side, bacon fried and not baked because everyone knows that baking is the boring way, and orange juice in tiny, real juice glasses.

"Where did you get these?" Ola wants to know.

"When my mom visited, she was appalled at how little I had in the way of kitchen things. Three weeks ago, I wouldn't have been able to properly feed you with just a plate and a bowl, more lost forks than found forks, and no little spoons. She took me shopping, and I had always liked the economy of those little glasses. They're barely three sips for me."

Ola can easily imagine Alex here with nothing because he left her most of the kitchen stuff. She doesn't remember now if it was because he thought he might come back, or because he had this new notion about traveling light.

Their exploration of Seattle is short-lived. The rain keeps sticking to Ola's glasses, and for periods of time, she sees the city through a filter of small water droplets. She votes they go somewhere to eat, and they take the streetcar just for the experience of it. Ola would have preferred to walk instead. She pays for lunch with a new debit card because the old one had expired, but she likes the impression that the scratch-free surface makes on Alex, who doesn't complain about her paying. Ola can't help but search for signs of relief on his forehead, the loosening up, the hairline falling a millimeter, but maybe she missed it.

When it's time to leave the city, Ola does not know how to ask Alex to come to Chicago, or even how to ask him if she can move to Seattle. They are both silently brooding over a few variations on these words. She stays an extra two hours for a slow nap in bed, like a real cuddle where the goal is to get close, to touch all limbs, to feel warm. Instead of sliding out of her body, she presses herself in, refusing to witness the sadness from somewhere up there.

Alex finally says, "I don't want you to leave."

"I don't want to, but I have to."

¢

As she closes the door on the apartment with Alex following her down to the car for final goodbyes, she remembers that inside her car, underneath the passenger seat is a box full of Alex's belongings. She won't tell him, though. The box will follow her back home.

CHAPTER SEVENTEEN

Laurie

Laurie can't go through with it. She sits on gum-caked concrete steps and watches the light on the corner changing, pedestrians jaywalking, and bikers running red lights. Her vision clouds over when she knows the cycle of that intersection by heart. The sun set hours ago. Wind swirls leaves and kicks up McDonald's garbage waiting to be covered by that first blanket of snow. It feels more desolate to Laurie, though, since she's about to hug a stranger in a bed that will likely be too firm, the pillows overstuffed, the blankets cool on the outside, warm on the inside.

She picked a new mattress with Mark when they moved to the city. Options were limited that day because they were choosing from the discount stack wrapped in plastic and waiting to be carried out of the store without fanfare. Mark let her have the final say, and she settled on a pillow-top that made her feel enveloped on all sides even through the plastic, which was no small feat. They strapped it to the roof of a borrowed sedan like an oversized bonnet on a tiny head. Every stop sign and red light forced them to question the tightness of the knots threatening to unravel.

She's late for this appointment with Jer, and she's watching the door. Soon Jer will open it a crack and look out for someone who could be his bedmate for the next two hours. His palms will sweat as he wonders if it could have been a joke or a police set-up. Craigslist is not known for its trustworthiness as a website.

Laurie won't be confirming or renewing Jer's faith in the anonymous ads that exploit emotional weakness in hundreds of people a day. She'll look for the top of his head and then she'll leave. One hundred and twenty dollars won't make or break her this week now that she has three employees, who have already followed through with their appointments.

It happens exactly as she imagined except that Jer has a full head of hair and sharp wide cheek bones that pair oddly with a solid, pointed chin marked by stubble. His eyes meet hers for a second before she looks down. A bus stopping behind a line of cars at the intersection ahead blocks his view of her, and Laurie takes that time to get up, brush off the back of her jeans, and join the streams of people walking to the train station.

It's too crowded for a seat so she wrestles her way to the back of the car where she can at least lean against the door without being disturbed. Her phone buzzes to let he know someone is texting. Michelle, most likely. She abandoned her on the night of her cuddling appointment. Fully aware of what she was doing, Laurie went to the movies with Mark on their first real date in weeks. It doesn't matter what they saw because all she remembers is the lasting warmth of his arm on half of the armrest. At her other side, Laurie felt her phone vibrating through her purse against her thigh. Now, all Michelle wants to do is drop off Laurie's share of the money. They both know she doesn't deserve it. But they choose a time (tomorrow, 10am) and a place (Mark's office). The least Laurie can do is go to where Michelle is. There's a tin taste in her mouth, too, like a bright new canker sore advertising its arrival.

¢

When Mark gets home from work later, Laurie asks him how to get to his office.

"You really don't remember," Mark responds from the kitchen.

"No." She is unabashed.

He turns away from her and starts preparing his dinner.

"I didn't cuddle," she says to smooth something over. If he can sense that she's ready, he can help her find out a more legitimate job, something that won't embarrass him in front of his parents if he even cares about that.

"Why do you need to go to my office?"

"I need to pick something up from Michelle."

"Money?" he asks without meeting her eyes.

"Yes."

"You know she had a really uncomfortable situation with her cuddling thing," he says coming back into the living room where she sits too stubborn to move where he is preparing himself a dinner for one.

"What do you mean?" Laurie asks because she doesn't think Mark saw those texts from Michelle. She finally has proof of communication between the two of them, but it isn't time to confront him yet. She wants more information to maximize the guilt he'll feel.

"She wanted to be extracted," he says.

"She should have texted then."

"She did." He drops the cover entirely. Laurie knows he wants her to know.

"We were on a date."

"It shouldn't have mattered."

He sleeps on the couch that night without any excuse or explanation, and Laurie comes out to offer the bed a little after midnight since she cannot get comfortable. The bedspread is too heavy and not heavy enough with cold and hot patches where they're not supposed to be.

"I don't want the bed," Mark says without uncovering his face, deliberately making himself difficult to understand.

"If you don't take it, I won't go back there."

"That's fine if you don't want to sleep."

"I'll be in the kitchen then if you want to talk." She doesn't know exactly if this is the right thing to say. Her parents were divorced long before she could really understand what sleeping on the couch meant, how it impacted even forced intimacy.

She turns the light on in the kitchen and pulls a stool up to the makeshift island where Mark left out a loaf of bread. She starts to pick at the crust—her favorite. The roof of her mouth protests first, followed by her throat. The bread is dry because it's old. She can't complain, though, because she didn't buy it, and she won't be the one to throw it away.

After an hour of keeping her eyes open against their will by reading anything in sight, Laurie gives up and walks back into the bedroom without glancing in the direction of the couch. It doesn't matter if Mark is asleep or if he's sitting up with his head cradled in his hands to ward off the guilt headache she imagines building behind his eyes. But she wonders if he's cold without the regular heaviness of their comforter and her body as a little furnace near enough to touch theoretically. Fractals form behind her eyelids in blues and greens. They speed up with her thoughts and slow down when she strains to hear his breathing out there.

¢

In the morning, they ride the Blue Line south and the Red Line back north, cursing the CTA's inconvenience but silently because they're not speaking anymore. She could've gone alone early or later, but she doesn't want Michelle to know anything has changed.

They walk through the door of his office almost an hour later, and Laurie breathes in the familiar smell that sticks to Mark's jacket. It's mostly warm food smell, like pasta doused in olive oil, and a little bit the smell of toner always busy in three big printers set against the back wall. The smell fits a place with so much sun-bleached wood.

They walk over to Michelle's desk. Thankfully, it's in a room separate from where Mark works even if she has a view of the back of his head when he's there working. She wonders if they rendezvous in the kitchen for planned water breaks.

"Where is she?" Laurie asks when they stop at the impersonal flat plane of her desk that still smells like disinfecting wipes. She doesn't keep mementos on it like the other employees. No pictures, no knick knacks, save for an empty glass.

"I don't know. She's usually right here." After a pause, "You want to meet my boss finally?"

"Will he give me a job?" Laurie asks louder than she knows she's supposed to.

"Quiet," he says and even quieter still, "At this point, I'm not sure why you would want that."

He leads her through the main room and some people acknowledge Laurie with a smile and a wave while others stare and blink quizzically until returning attention to a phone call or computer screen. She was never a fixture here.

The boss's office is sprawling and rich with modern furniture and deep rugs she could sink her whole body into. He stands from his desk with a hand extended.

"I'm Lucas," he says.

"This is Laurie," Mark says before Laurie can do it herself.

"To what do we owe the honor?" He's so polite that Laurie wouldn't flinch if he bent forward to kiss her hand. Tactics like these are what she needs to find some investors.

"I'm looking for Michelle. She and I are partners in a little business venture I'm starting."

"Mostly I just wanted to show Laurie the office after the re-model," Mark says, and Laurie knows he's trying to steer the conversation away.

"Michelle isn't here right now."

Laurie feels a jolt. She's taken the money and run. She's the first in a long line of people who Laurie will only want to refer to as a high turnover rate for cuddlers. The biggest flaw in her business model: people who get cold feet and decide that the whole thing is too personal to be impersonal. No shows will lead to bad reviews online eventually outweighing the success stories.

"Why?" Mark asks, sharply. Laurie knows she shouldn't want to see this. He's not a test subject whose movements can be measured, observed, and logged for review at a later date. If Michelle shows up and his shoulders soften, she'll know. She'll know by the tone of his voice, and the way he'll choose his words more carefully, like she suspects one might in a job interview. It'll be all the proof she needs.

"She asked me if she could go out and buy some real breakfast." Lucas raises his arms to put the word "real" in scare quotes. "Kind of insulting, but if she's having a bad enough day to crave carbs then who am I to stop her? Want me to let her know you stopped by?"

"No. We'll wait," Laurie says.

"Shouldn't be too long."

"The new additions to the office are beautiful." Laurie sees the opportunity here to ask for a job, but she can't take it. It wouldn't sound right coming out of her mouth shaped as it is into a tense line.

While Lucas goes back to work or whatever passes for work when you're the owner of a small company that basically runs itself, another silence fills the space between Laurie and Mark on the couch.

¢

No one sees her when she leaves the office alone. Over in the park across the street, she takes a slim corner of a bench and pulls out her phone. "Do we even need to say it?" is what she types to him. She receives no response even though she can almost feel him staring through the wide pane of glass in the office's kitchen. If she had anything to say, she would keep typing to see how long it took to get him to come down, ask her to stop, make some sort of a scene.

She imagines the apartment she could afford without Mark: sloping floors, bathroom the size of her mom's linen closet with barely enough room to turn a circle in front of the mirror. But what would really get to her would be the echo of the new place bare without art, furniture, textile. Friends, even though she'd never admit to the breakup openly, would call and tell immediately that something was different. The room's tone would draw out the conversation's content. They would expect her to cry, but she knows she wouldn't be able to do that for a long time.

And she really should stop using the conditional here. Over the last fourteen hours something shifted, maybe when she sat in the kitchen, maybe when she refused to look his way that night, maybe he was on the verge of saying sorry. The words could have been caught in his throat like they were caught in hers even now. Or she's still trying to piece it together because memory is fucking difficult and she's already twisting what happened to suit her aims/her way of thinking about how to think of Mark. Right now, she's interested in the role of wounded victim for herself. She remembers how he told her she was grasping at straws with all of these jobs. She remembers the shore of smooth Lake Michigan peeking at her through the gaps in apartment buildings. How lucky it would be to walk into any one of them with the keys to something breezy on the eighth floor. How lucky it would have been for anyone to see the potential in what she was doing.

ACKNOWLEDGMENTS

The author would like to thank her family, classmates, professors, and Micah—all of whom had great influence over what appears between the covers of this book.

ABOUT THE AUTHOR

Magdalena Waz's fiction and essays have appeared in *Threadcount, The Collagist,* and *Rabbit Catastrophe Review.* She holds an MA in Creative Writing from Miami University (Ohio) and currently lives in Brooklyn.

58588319R00097

Made in the USA
Lexington, KY
14 December 2016